CLOSER

THE UNIT
BOOK ONE

BESTSELLING AUTHOR
SARAH GREYSON

CLOSER

Cover Design by Lori Follett with Wicked Book Covers

Editing by Laura Donohue

Interior Design and Formatting by Fancypants Book Formatting

Sarah Greyson

Visit my webpage: www.sarahgreyson.com

SARAH GREYSON

CONTENTS

CLOSER

He had killed many men. He had killed women and even a few children. He had seen people die right in front of him. They would bleed out from a gunshot wound. They would have their insides blown out from a high-caliber bullet. They would blow up in a roadside bomb, limbs flying high in the air.

He didn't regret what he did or what he'd seen because it had been in the name of war. Still the images haunted him. Every day was another day filled with death and dismemberment. The demons, the ones he could never quite catch, the ones he could never quite kill, the ones responsible for the carnage, plagued him.

He never told his fellow Unit members of the death scenes that constantly ran through his mind. They were strong. He was weak because death, dismemberment, and beheadings bothered him so. He couldn't talk about it without his eyes filling with tears. He'd tried when he first got out of the Army three months ago. He went to see a therapist, but he soon realized that she would never understand what he'd seen and experienced in his five deployments to Iraq and Afghanistan as a Green Beret.

He was released from the military but not from the torment. He stared at his right hand as he tried to hold it steady. His career in the Army taught him to be a steady, straight shot. He worried now that that was gone as he looked at his hand shaking uncontrollably. He willed it to stop, but it didn't.

Rubbing his hands over his jeans, he stood and made his way to his kitchen where he poured four-fingers of scotch–the cure for what ailed him.

In the days since his release, he had tried to socialize with people. He had tried to re-acclimate to society. When he went out, he swore people were following him. Or, after getting drunk, he would have to acquire small things, like a knife for protection, from the places he visited. Or he would drive recklessly, not because of the alcohol, but because he knew he had to outrun the car behind him. He almost caused several accidents. He would have had he not been trained in defensive driving.

Although his mother had raised a gentleman, he no longer behaved like one. He had needs after all, so he went to the clubs and local bars. He was a good-looking man and never had any trouble getting the hottest women. But the girls he brought to his apartment were always small and fragile. Not his type at all.

He didn't know why he kept bringing the fragile girls home. Maybe he just needed to be someone's hero for the night. He had to hold back with the girls he brought to his apartment or he would break them. He would hurt them if he unleashed the animal that lived inside him. So he fucked them but remained unsatisfied.

It was official, he had become an antisocial bastard. Not at all the man he was before he went to war as a Green Beret.

He plopped himself back down on his old, brown recliner and gulped his scotch. *What was he going to do?* He'd been out three months, and the sight of a car behind him made him anxious. He'd become paranoid and constantly felt on edge. He was hyper vigilant of the sounds and sights around him.

His gaze shifted to his closed blinds. He didn't want to see outside, and he didn't want anyone seeing in. He needed to stay inside where he felt safe, in control. Lying on his side table was his firearm. He never left home without it.

Just the other day, as he pushed his shopping cart down the grocery store aisle, he heard a baby crying. He became so irritated that he drove his cart directly to the checkout and had the clerk ring up his five items: Spaghetti-Ohs, Frosted Mini-Wheats, milk, bread, and one pound of lunchmeat. He tapped his fingers anxiously on the counter as he looked around, waiting on the cashier. Looking outside, he noticed the same green sedan that was behind him on his way to the store. He reached behind him and felt his gun tucked safely in the waistband of his jeans. Just knowing he had it brought him a sense of comfort. But that and scotch were the only things to bring him comfort these days.

He shifted the cell phone to his right ear. "I know, Mom. I will," he said impatiently.

"I just don't understand why you won't come over for dinner, honey. We miss you. Now that you're home, we haven't seen you but twice in three months, Michael. You know your father and I miss you greatly."

Oh, she was really laying it on thick.

"Okay, Mom. I know. When do you want me over?"

"How's Sunday night? I'll make your favorite: chicken-fried steak with mashed potatoes and the white gravy you love so much."

"Fine," Michael gritted through clenched teeth. He couldn't drink when he went to see his parents. The last thing he wanted to do was worry them. So he drank alone.

"Okay, Mom. I'll see you Sunday . . . I love you, too." He tossed his cell phone on the chair as he stood, making his way to the kitchen for another drink. The splashing of the liquid into the glass did wonders for him. He had to calm his mind. He had to slow it down. These days, it was in constant motion with images and thoughts of trying to save all of the lives he lost, all of the lives he took.

Michael was a good man. He knew that somewhere deep down. But blood covered the goodness that once existed. And war buried the rest.

As he poured the amber liquid down his throat, he thought about how it would feel to become invisible. He wanted to disappear into the death that was his world.

CLOSER

SARAH GREYSON

CHAPTER ONE

"Get out!" Leroy shouted. *Michael was almost finished rigging the last bomb, set to blow up one of the Al-Qaeda base camps. "Get out! They're coming fast."*

Michael could feel the zing of the bullets narrowly missing his head. A little more to the left and half of his face would have been gone. Michael stood to his full height of six-foot-two and headed towards the door of the compact mud building.

"Leroy? Which direction are they holding?" Michael shouted.

"The east. We have to get behind that house." Leroy pointed to a compact mud hut with holes in the walls that served as windows as he continued to supply cover fire. "We'll rendezvous with the others there."

"Cover me," Michael yelled to Leroy.

Michael ran for the hut as Leroy sprayed bullets to the east. He made it to the house and turned back to lay down cover fire for Leroy through a hole in the building. Michael fired as Leroy sprinted to him. He heard it before he saw it. The homemade explosive resounded through the dust that swirled like a cloud in front of Michael. When the dust cleared, Michael saw him. Not five feet from him, Leroy lay on the packed desert ground, blood spilling from his stomach. A piece of his intestine hung loosely to the left of the hole the 762.54 caliber bullet exit wound left in his body armor. An Al-Qaeda extremist armed with a Russian Squad automatic rifle had shot his brother in the back. There would be no way to save Leroy from the damage that high caliber bullet caused, but he had to try.

Out of the twelve-man team Michael was deployed with, he and Leroy, along with a few others, had served five tours together. He had to reach him. He laid down fire with his weapon while he ran into the open space between the buildings. He grabbed Leroy by the shoulder strap of his rifle and started to drag him behind the building. He needed the medic.

Michael pulled Leroy to safety and peered through the hole in the wall, watching for the armed extremists. He stared in horror when he saw a little boy, no more than ten years old, walk into the midst of the gunfire. The boy just stood there, eyes filled with fear, as bullets whizzed by. Michael motioned for the boy to take cover, but the boy stood still. Watching in anguish, Michael saw the crying boy lift his right hand. Michael's eyes were glued to the detonator, about to be activated by only a child.

Michael bolted straight up in his bed. Sweat was dripping from his face and body. Thank goodness he'd taken to sleeping naked or his clothes would have been wrecked. Another nightmare. Another sleepless night.

He got out of bed, meandered into the kitchen, and flipped the light switch, hoping to chase the shadows away. Needing to rid his mind of the ingrained image of that ten-year-old boy, Michael reached up above his refrigerator and grabbed the bottle of scotch. He pulled down a glass from the cupboard and poured himself four fingers. Walking into his living room to his favorite recliner, he sat down and took a nice, long swallow. Grabbing the remote control, he flipped through the stations trying to decide which infomercial to watch at 0100 hours. This was quickly becoming his routine: try to sleep, have nightmare, drink scotch, pass out.

The sun rose and glared through the blinds. Michael lifted his head to an aching throb and a stiff neck. He squinted at the sunlight that managed to make its way into the living room. He remembered looking at the clock at 0400 and watching part of the "Snuggie" infomercial. He must have passed out in his chair. His body would pay for it today during his run.

He got up and headed into the kitchen, a small galley with just enough space for one person to stand. Counter space was non-existent. There was a breakfast bar above the sink that separated the kitchen from the living room. Six months out of the military. This was his life. He wished his father hadn't given his life for America so he could talk to him about the horrors of war. His dad would understand. *Who else did he really have to talk to that would understand war?* He couldn't talk to his teammates—they were all tough men and surely not suffering like he was. He would never admit to his suffering anyways.

His brother wouldn't understand, not that he would even care. Justin was so dedicated to the almighty dollar of Wall Street that when Michael finished with the service, Justin didn't even bother to visit him. Being the younger brother, Michael was lucky Justin called him at all, no doubt after a guilt trip laid on him by their mother.

Michael's mother, on the other hand, thanked God the day her baby came home for good. She'd been so frightened his life would end the same way her husband's did. Part of Michael wished his life had ended in Afghanistan so he wouldn't have to relive the war in his mind day and night.

He fidgeted around with the coffee pot, placing a filter inside the basket and scooping in the coffee. Advil and coffee were the best cures he had found for his hangovers. Drinking during the day was not his thing. Not yet anyways.

Halfway through his first cup of coffee there was a knock at the door. It was only 0700. Someone better have a damn good reason to be at his house so early, while he still felt like shit. His training had him grabbing for his 9mm Beretta before laying his hand on the doorknob. He placed the gun at his side as he opened the door.

"Michael," sighed Rob.

"Rob, man, what the fuck? What are you doing here so early?" he demanded as he walked back into his kitchen and placed his gun on the counter.

Rob ran a hand roughly over his stubble and then through his hair. He fidgeted, scratching his forearm with his long fingers. Michael never remembered seeing Rob so agitated. To be a Green Beret meant a soldier was always steady under pressure. They had only been out for six months. He hadn't forgotten how to be cool under pressure after eight years of service. He doubted Rob had either.

"I have a job I thought you might be interested in," Rob explained walking into Michael's apartment.

"What? And it couldn't wait until a decent hour?"

"No, man, the client is in a big hurry. Wants it done yesterday." Rob peeked out the living room window. *Was he looking for someone? Was someone following him?*

Michael considered Rob one of his closest friends. More like a brother than his own. Michael would do anything for Rob, and Rob knew it. They had served together on five tours in Afghanistan, together with four other men—Tony, Steve, Kevin, and Leroy. All of the men, with the exception of Leroy, left the Army at the same time and had aspirations of making it big in the private security sector. Most of the jobs they took paid well enough but were limited contracts: Guarding a celebrity, providing security detail for a diplomat while in a foreign country.

Michael had taken three jobs, and all of them had come through Rob. Rob had connections at Blackrain

Security, and they wanted to bring Rob, Michael, Steve, and Tony in to work strictly for them. But Rob hadn't yet convinced his brothers. Lately, Rob had been so sidetracked he failed to check in with Michael over the last week. Rob had a nasty shrapnel scar on his leg from when the Humvee in front of theirs blew up. Rob was the medic, but every Green Beret was trained in two jobs. If one man went down, another man was there to take his place. Michael's medical cross-training with Rob was what saved Rob's leg and his life. Rob felt like he owed Michael for saving his leg, and Michael knew it. In truth, Michael loved the guy, so his dying was not an option.

"What's the job?" Michael asked.

"The client wants you to kidnap a scientist with ties to the Armed Islamic Group known as the GIA," Rob disclosed as he paced back and forth in front of Michael's flat screen television that hung on the wall opposite the recliner.

"Kidnap? What the fuck? That's not what we do," Michael warned.

"But this scientist is going to help the GIA with a new breed of weapon. We have to stop it, Michael. After all we've done for our country, we can't quit now. After all of the men we watched die, after losing Leroy. Just because we're out of the military doesn't mean our love and duty to our country stops. You know that," Rob concluded.

"How much does it pay?" After all, if Michael was going to go to jail, it was going to be for something worth his while.

16

"Two hundred grand," Rob said, plopping himself down onto Michael's faded hand-me-down couch.

"When will I get the details?" Michael asked as he considered taking the job even though kidnapping could land him in jail. Still, the thought of a new breed of weapon in the hands of the terrorists was more worrisome than some jail time.

"They'll be sent via courier tomorrow at 0700."

This time it was Michael who was pacing. "Why don't you take the job if it pays so much?" Michael questioned.

"My bum leg," Rob replied. "You know I can't move like I used to, not with my muscle damaged from the shrapnel."

"Fine, but I want to see half the money in my account before I make any moves," Michael conceded.

"Same account?" Rob raised his eyebrows.

Michael nodded. He could do a lot with two hundred grand. Move out of his shit-hole apartment for one thing. He'd been saving money to buy a cabin in the Sugarloaf Mountains. The mountains held his fondest memories. Memories of skiing and laughing with his father.

Rob stopped pacing and rushed to Michael, extending his hand. When Michael took it, he pulled him into a one-arm hug. "Thank you, man! You have no idea what this means to me."

"It's just a job, man, calm down," Michael said as he cautiously backed away from Rob's embrace.

"I know. I just really needed you to take this job. It will be an easy two hundred grand. That should set you up real nice. Then I'll feel like I'm paying down my debt to you."

"Whatever, man. You know I don't expect anything from you. If it had been me lying there, you would've done the same thing. You don't owe me anything," Michael said as they walked to the door.

Rob bumped fists with Michael and disappeared down the stairs, while Michael shut the door and returned to his coffee.

Later, as he pulled out his laptop to verify the money had been deposited in his account, Michael couldn't shake his feeling of apprehension. Why would Rob be so happy he took this job or that he was the one making all of the money? *Maybe Rob was getting a kickback.* Michael made his way over to the same window Rob was focused on earlier and peeked outside. The only thing Michael noticed were the heavy, gray storm clouds that blocked out the sun.

CHAPTER TWO

Emma sat at her desk writing notes on her current prototype. It was her fourth design over the last year. The first had failed to hover. The second would fly, but the neuromorphic processors located in the bird's brain would not initiate a turn. The third was fully functional. Still it failed to deliver the chemical agent when the artificial intelligence recognized its target.

She had designed the robot, no bigger than a hummingbird, with the latest nanotechnology—a silicon chip designed by the Germans to allow it to fly all on its own. No one had to man a control station or press a button when it was time to release the agent. The hummingbird had a programmable chip that was capable of imitating the human brain by running complex processes at the same time, much like the way neurons fired in the brain. This chip was placed inside the bird's brain and operated the bird. Key to the operation was the bird's ability to run facial recognition software simultaneously with other processes. In this manner, the CIA and the DOD would work together. The CIA would provide intelligence on known terrorists in a cell, and the DOD would program the bird with the information. The artificial intelligence would determine its target and deploy the chemical agent.

Failing to deploy this agent was a major flaw in the design, and Emma had to find it. This last step was crucial to finishing on deadline, which was fast approaching. She had to figure out a way for the nozzle of the spray tube to deploy through the belly of the bird and release the pharmacological agent into the air as a fine mist upon the bird's recognition of the target.

Her work, dubbed Project Hummingbird, was Top Secret. Only a handful of people knew of the project's existence, including a few top military members of the DOD and some high level agents with the CIA. There was a huge black market for the kind of weapon she was developing. If the wrong person got their hands on her research, it could have major implications in the war on terror. This was the first weapon of its kind, and Emma, at twenty-eight, was granted the honor to develop it. Of course, because it was her brainchild, she spent many hours talking her project up to the right people.

She had graduated at the top of her class from the University of Maine earning a dual PhD in Mechanical Engineering and Bio-Chemical Engineering. She had worked long, hard hours to get this assignment. When she was awarded the position, she had achieved one of her life-long goals: to design and implement artificial intelligence for use against America's enemies.

Her father had worked for the DOD his entire career and made it his mission to keep America safe from foreign and domestic threats. Her parents had since retired to Skowhegan, Maine, a smaller town about an hour away from Emma. She still visited them every chance she got. However, with her schedule, visits weren't frequent. Since she was their only child, her parents still doted over her. They would send her care packages, and her mother would include fresh baked peanut butter cookies—Emma's favorite. She loved her parents, and it was because of her dad that she had landed in her current position with the DOD. He was a well-respected scientist and had pulled some strings to get her foot in the door. Still, the rest was up to her. She had to earn the trust and respect of her superiors, plus maintain an impeccable reputation in order to work on this Top Secret project.

Emma's research and subsequent work would be invaluable in stopping terrorist groups dead in their tracks. And the best part was that the pharmacological agent to be released rendered the subjects incapacitated for eight hours. Plenty of time for the military to move in and collect the terrorists without causing any casualties. The DOD was anxious for her to complete her work and provide them with a working Hummingbird. Once the prototype was tested, the DOD and the CIA could begin work on manufacturing the bird and stop the terrorists without killing them, which would allow for more interrogations and intelligence gathering.

According to a U.N. Report she had read, America was one of only four countries with this type of nanotechnology project underway. America, Israel,

South Korea, and the UK were all in a race of sorts. Her Hummingbird would not cause suffering to any civilian populations. God knew there was enough controversy over the current Drone program.

After Emma had been at it for a good four hours, Bethany popped her head into her office. "Emma, it's almost lunch time. Want to run down to the Cornerstone Deli and grab a sandwich? We can catch up."

Bethany, her college roommate, worked in the same building as Emma. How they managed to swing that, she would never truly know. *What were the odds?* Emma's dad knew how brilliant Bethany was, and Emma suspected he was able to get Bethany a job as well. They were not allowed to discuss their work with anyone, let alone each other. Her former roommate was a bit of a gossip and a busybody and was always trying to get information out of Emma. Emma was strong though, always effectively changing the subject with each attempt Bethany made.

It had been over a week since they had any girl time. Emma was long overdue for some much needed distractions, and Bethany was always good for some fun. Emma could clear her mind and come back with a fresh perspective.

"Sure," Emma replied. "Let me grab my coat."

It was bitterly cold in Lewiston, Maine this time of the year. Thankfully, the holidays were over. Now was the long wait for spring. Somewhere in Punxsutawney, Pennsylvania a groundhog named "Punxsutawney Phil" had seen his shadow, which meant six more weeks of winter. While Emma loved the snow, she was growing tired of the cold weather. If only she wasn't working under a deadline, she would take a vacation to the glow and hospitality of Cancun. She'd invite Bethany and Ashley and make it a girls' getaway. They could sit on the beach, or better yet, the poolside bar, and drink their cares away. What a nice dream. She had three weeks left before she had to submit a fully functioning Hummingbird. Perhaps after her deadline, she'd take her much deserved getaway. She'd make plans today, while at lunch with Bethany. She knew, without asking, that Ashley would be game for a trip.

Emma and Bethany took the stairs down four flights. Emma tried to take the stairs as much as possible to shed the extra twenty pounds she'd put on. Standing at five foot eight, her weight had been holding steady at one hundred sixty pounds. She desperately wanted to lose those extra pounds and get back to her pre-stress weight. She did not, however, have time to exercise. That was her excuse.

The truth was that by the time Emma got home from her extra-long days at the office, all she wanted to do was to curl up with the latest romance novel and dream her night away. If she couldn't find a real romance, she certainly could find one in her dreams. She was good at escaping into her fictional characters' worlds. She loved the intensity and dalliance she found in her book boyfriends. They always treated her right and, most importantly, mentally stimulated her. That was the reason she quit dating before she'd been awarded this project. She'd find a guy who was mentally stimulating but did nothing for her in the chemistry department. Or she'd find someone she was attracted to, but he could not arouse her mind. So, she devoted herself to her work. Everything else would just have to wait.

Reaching the bottom of the stairs, they turned right to the security desk. "Hi, Paul. I need my things. I'm headed out," she said to the security officer. He handed her purse and cell phone to her. She shoved her cell phone into her purse and pushed open the door. Stepping outside, the cold air smacked her in the face. She was so ready for spring. Tightening her coat around her, she crossed her arms in front of her body and tucked her hands under her arms. She walked, head down, to the Cornerstone Deli in comfortable silence with Bethany.

They reached the Deli and placed their order. Emma behaved and ordered a turkey and veggie sandwich minus the bag of chips with a water to drink. Bethany, God love her, had the metabolism of an eighteen-year-old. She could eat whatever her heart desired and not gain a pound. She had the perfect figure—one the guys couldn't get enough of. Where Bethany had long blonde hair that curled loosely over her shoulders, Emma had wavy, dark auburn, shoulder length hair that she always wore in a chignon. Bethany also had the height of a model, a cool five foot ten with killer legs. Not that Emma was jealous. Emma was just so competitive, she didn't like looking up to anyone.

"So, how's work going?" Bethany inquired, sitting herself down at a table nearest the large display window looking out onto the street.

"You know I can't talk about work. Why do you always ask? Don't you have any juicy stories to tell me so I can live vicariously through you?" Emma asked, smiling brightly at her friend.

"Since you asked, because you know I wouldn't have brought it up otherwise, there is something," Bethany responded.

Yeah, right.

"I went out last night with Aaron. It was our second date," Bethany taunted. "He could not keep his hands to himself. I finally had to tell him enough was enough, and I wasn't interested in taking it any further than second base. I let him feel me up, but that was it."

Bethany still used middle-school terms to describe her sexual escapades. And God knew there were a great number of them. Bethany wasn't a slut. She just truly enjoyed the company of men.

"So, how was he? Was he a good kisser?" Emma wondered as she took a bite of her turkey and veggie sandwich.

"No, God, he was awful. For such a good-looking man, he had a drooling problem. I almost gagged."

"Then why did you let him continue?" Emma wondered as she put down her sandwich and wiped at her mouth.

"Because I didn't want to be rude," Bethany explained.

For such a brilliant girl, Bethany could really be stupid at times. The conversation continued on and reached its inevitable conclusion of Bethany politely declining a third date with the man.

"In a month or so, want to take a trip to Cancun? Just you, me, and Ashley?" Emma inquired.

Bethany shoved her last bite into her mouth and exclaimed, "Hell yeah!"

"Great! I'll talk to Ashley and then make the arrangements," Emma said, sipping her water. "I'll let you know how much, and we can narrow down the dates. I want to do it soon though. Deal?" Emma asked.

"Deal!" Bethany declared, slurping the last bit of her Diet Coke through her straw.

Emma was not at all looking forward to going outside. From the front window of the Deli she could see the biting cold wind blowing the dust and debris around in circles on the street.

As Emma sat listening to Bethany go on about what she was going to wear on her newest date with a man she had just met at a club the previous weekend, the hair on the back of her nape stood on end. An uneasy feeling washed over her. She looked around. She could feel someone watching her. She knew they probably had spies watching her high-security building, so it wasn't out of the realm of possibility she was being followed. Emma did not get to where she was by relying solely on her instincts. No. Emma had a brain, and by God, she used it.

She looked out of the window and only noticed the regular lunch crowd on their way to and from the downtown office buildings. Nothing seemed out of order. She was just paranoid. Maybe it was just a draft from the door opening with a new rush of people. That would clearly explain the chill that came over her. Still, what about the feeling that someone was watching her? *Maybe she had an admirer.* Now she was just being silly.

"Are you ready? I need to get back to work," Emma said uneasily as she started to stand, her gaze still riveted to the streets outside the building. Absentmindedly, she grabbed for her coat.

"What are you looking for?" Bethany wondered as she stood up with Emma, shrugging on her own jacket.

They threw their trash away and walked out into the blustery, cold weather, tightening their arms around their middles, effectively hugging themselves. Emma wanted to get away from the deli and back to the sanctuary that was her office and laboratory.

She was being watched. She knew that if anyone found out about her project, she would be the prime target for a kidnapping. The knowledge she had was valuable and more than enough for a terrorist to come after her. It was a good thing that only those with top secret, special access programs clearances had knowledge of Project Hummingbird.

She tried to justify her uneasiness. The DOD had put a security tail on her. That was all. Still, Emma walked faster, and Bethany, with her long legs, had no trouble keeping up. Finally, they made it into their building, throwing open the door, proceeding back to the security guard's desk.

"Here are my things, Paul. I should be out of here tonight around 7:00." She handed him her purse and cell phone to be placed in lockup. Emma began to relax, the feeling of being watched subsiding. "That was weird," Emma mumbled as she made her way to the stairs.

"What was?" Bethany inquired.

As they walked up the four flights to Emma's floor, she told Bethany how she felt like someone had been watching her. Bethany told her she was just being paranoid.

"After all, who would be stalking you?"

Bethany scoffed. Boy she could be rude.

"You're right." Emma sighed as she opened the door to her busy floor. People were milling about working on their projects. Emma told Bethany she'd talk to her later and let the door close safely behind her. She entered the safety and security of her lab.

Michael had never seen a creature so beautiful in his life, and she was working for a terrorist group? What was the world coming to? He received his package via courier that morning. In it was a picture of Emma Welby, along with her vital statistics. He decided the best course of action was to watch her routine. He could figure out her most vulnerable point and take her then. He'd followed her from her office to the deli where she and her friend had had lunch. He'd watched through the window as they laughed and talked with each other.

They were good friends, anyone could tell by their parallel body language. Even the way they'd hugged themselves in the cold was the same. They loved each other. That was obvious. They invaded each other's personal space with an ease of longtime friends as they huddled together for their trek back to their office.

He'd watched as she entered her building but lost sight of her at the stairwell. His intel didn't say what floor she worked on, only the building's name. He'd arrived ahead of time to make sure he didn't miss her going into the building. He'd been granted with her beauty a second time when she made her way to the deli. He couldn't believe he was actually attracted to a mark. She had the confidence and poise of a sophisticated lady. Something about her called out to him, and at the same time, brought him a sense of comfort. For the first time since returning home from the service, he actually felt like he had something to look forward to. She wasn't some stick figure model type that was all looks and no brain. No, it was clear that Emma Welby was much, much more.

Michael tried to remind himself that she was strictly a paycheck and a way to keep America safe, but even in doing so, he couldn't shake her allure. She was so vibrant, so beautiful. The way pieces of her auburn hair blew in the wind. The way her finger curled to tuck the runaway strand behind her ear. The way her arms snaked around her body. The sexy-as-fuck glasses she wore, which made her look all sorts of intelligent.

He instinctually knew, if given the chance, he could unleash his inner animal with her. He wouldn't have to hold back while fucking her. Knowing he wouldn't break her body or her will turned him on like nobody else ever had. Emma Welby was all woman, not some fragile girl. The thought of being with her aroused him like nothing he had ever experienced. The thought of fucking her relentlessly, of knowing she could take what he gave her and relish in his power, excited him. His mind was filled with thoughts of their first time together. Him pulling her hair, tilting her head back, looking deep into her eyes as he took her with his mouth. How would she taste?

Yes, she got to him. She did it for him. Just the sight of her caused him to crave her like a drug addict craves his next fix. She was the one with whom he could truly be himself.

He shook his head. He had to get a grip. She was the enemy. She was out to hurt his country. The country that he loved. The country he sacrificed his soul to protect. No, Emma was not the one for him. He'd worked too hard and too long serving his nation. He had to stop her before it was too late.

Still the thoughts crept into his mind like the blackness of night, blocking out all other. Maybe, just maybe, he could save her. Maybe, just maybe, he could have her for himself.

CHAPTER
THREE

He waited, huddled in his parked car. Every hour
or so he got out and placed money in the parking
meter. The last thing he needed was a parking ticket
indicating he'd been outside of her place of
employment. He was parked far enough away that no
one paid him any mind. Using the downtime to plan
and review his intel, he decided to follow her home and
wait until she was relaxed. Then he would take her.

She exited the building at 1900 hours. She had
both an apartment in the city and a cabin in the
mountains. *Where would they be going tonight?*

It was dark, which made it easier for him to
follow her unseen. Spotting her red Subaru Forester
exiting the parking garage, he pulled out from his spot
and followed a few cars behind her in his Jeep Grand
Cherokee. Spending time in the mountains necessitated
his need for the four-by-four vehicle, and he was damn
lucky. He was going to need it tonight if his suspicions
were correct. He carefully stayed several car lengths
behind her. About two hours later, she was pulling into
her driveway, which went up to her weekend cabin in
the Sugarloaf Mountains. This girl had everything he
wanted. She had a killer body. She had a killer mind.

She had a cabin in the mountains—a cabin like he was saving money to buy.

Michael parked at the base of the driveway, pulling out of sight behind some thick evergreen trees. He made his way, by foot, to her A-frame log cabin. The front was nothing but high windows. She must have an incredible view of the mountains from her home, he thought. He bet she loved it there. He would. He enjoyed the outdoors, and the Sugarloaf Mountains were his playground. He loved fishing in the streams and lakes in the spring, he loved hunting in the winter, and he loved boating in the lake in the summer. He especially loved the way the evergreen branches, thick with fallen snow, looked like a winter wonderland. There was nothing as comfortable as a wood burning fire in the winter. The smoke billowing from the chimney. The smell of the fire. The smell of the snow. The smell of home.

He perched outside the back of her home, waiting until she settled in for the evening. Thank goodness his training had prepared him to be patient and prepared in any circumstance. Some would call the training abuse. What could he say? He took it willingly. At any time he could have quit, but he wanted to be a Green Beret more than anything else in his life. He was extremely physically fit, had passed all of the tests, even some of the more rigorous ones designed to break the strongest of men.

The night was cold, but it didn't affect him. He felt his Beretta against his forearm as he squatted and peered through Emma's kitchen window. He would bide his time and wait for the perfect opportunity. Not wanting to rush such an expensive and important mission, kidnapping a person loyal to the GIA, he patiently waited in the bitterly cold temperatures. He was lucky if the thermometer read nine degrees. Add in the wind-chill factor, and he was sure it was negative nine. He did, however, have a fantastic view of the surrounding mountains. He looked behind him and admired the glow of the moon, the way the moonlight lit the tops of the trees in the forest that surrounded Emma's cabin.

Her lights were on, but it was dark outside, which gave him the perfect view inside her home. He noticed her make her way upstairs and turn on the bedroom light. *Thank God she didn't have a single curtain on any window.* She undressed and pulled on her pajama bottoms and a tank top. He watched, mesmerized by the sight of her figure in the window. He could see her ample bosom. He liked a woman with large breasts, but there was something more to her than just her breasts. He was drawn to her. There was something about her body that had his aching for her touch. How was he going to survive this kidnapping? He just had to keep reminding himself she was working for the bad guys.

She turned off her bedroom light and made her way back downstairs. She walked into her spacious kitchen and poured herself something to drink. Then she made her way into the living room, took out her laptop, and sat on the couch. He watched as she pulled an old afghan over her legs and brought her laptop to her lap. She was finally relaxing into the false security of her cabin retreat.

Michael waited for forty-five minutes before he approached the back door. With his lock-picking tools, he entered her kitchen in a matter of seconds. It was spacious with wooden cabinets and a U-shaped counter top, which doubled as a breakfast bar. The exposed oak beams of her ceiling were high and steeped and ran throughout the kitchen and, he assumed, the rest of the house. On top of the kitchen sat a quiet little loft with a banister as a half wall. That was where her bedroom was located. He could tell from the layout of the windows.

He moved quietly past the kitchen table and hid himself behind the stone-faced hearth of her fireplace located in the center of the room. Emma remained on the sofa, unaware. Blond hardwood floors ran throughout the cabin. He could see the growth rings of the trees, which told him he wasn't looking at laminate but at real hardwood. She must make a pretty penny to afford this home. The walls were a rich, burnt orange color that accented the floors.

He pulled his gun quietly from his side holster and approached her. She was engrossed in her laptop and oblivious to his body moving quietly. He stood a foot away from her when he first spoke.

"Be still," he commanded.

She jumped up, dropping her laptop to the floor, and scrambled to the farthest corner of the couch. Their eyes connected, and he felt it to his very core. She lit a fire in him that had long since been dormant. He felt his inner animal call out to her. He moved closer, aiming the gun at her head.

Emma couldn't believe her eyes. There was a strange man standing in her living room, pointing a gun at her? Her mind went to her intel. Was he a terrorist? She wanted to voice her questions, but she was too terrified to speak. She hugged herself, trying to sink into the couch and away from this stranger with a gun.

In his peripheral vision, he noticed a wet bar and fully stocked wine case. *What's her favorite flavor of wine? Whoa! Where did that come from? She works for the bad guys, remember?*

"What do you want," Emma asked coolly, as she cowered against the side arm of her couch.

"I want you to get up slowly and move into the kitchen," he said.

Across from the red leather couch she was cowering on sat an identical coach, both facing each other and perpendicular to the fireplace. Her furniture was new, not like his hand-me-downs. *The terrorist business must pay well.* Still, he couldn't help but admire her sitting there on her couch.

Emma did as he bid. She rose, and he moved closer to her. He was now wedged between the coffee table and the couch, standing less than a foot in front of her. Nerve endings were firing all over his body. He could feel the pull of his groin. She was affecting him in the most primal of ways. He growled and flicked his gun at her, indicating for her to move past him and into the kitchen. He didn't want to feel this way for her.

Emma did as she was told. She didn't want to upset him. She had to keep things calm. Still, when he neared her body, she felt tingles travel down her spine. She had never experienced such a sensation from being near a man before. She rationalized it must be the adrenaline coursing through her veins. As she brushed past him, she touched him and a bolt of energy made her clit throb. It had to be adrenaline. She was not attracted to him. How could she be? He was pointing a gun at her.

He didn't move as she brushed past, electrifying him with the barest of touches. He followed her into the kitchen and commanded her to sit down. She lowered herself to sit upon her kitchen chair. He pulled open the duffle bag he'd stored by the kitchen door and pulled out rope.

She had delicate porcelain skin. She wore no make-up but still she was the most beautiful creature he had ever laid eyes on. Her dark auburn hair fell around her shoulders. Her demure nose accented her deep blue eyes. She had the fullest, naturally red pouty lips he had ever seen. She wore those sexy, stylish glasses, which did not detract from her penetrating eyes. Her ass was a little bigger, especially at the hips, just the way he liked his women—curvy. She was definitely doing something to him. His erection was pushing against his dark pants.

"What do you want?" she asked again, sitting still in the chair, mindful his gun was pointed directly at her head.

He approached her with the rope. He knelt behind her and caught her scent. She smelled of earthy goodness mixed with lavender. He felt heady from the need she was creating within him. He could not bring himself to mark her perfect porcelain skin, so he tied her hands more loosely than he normally would have, still making sure they were secure and bound behind her back. He would have a gun on her the whole time anyway.

"What do you want?" she demanded again, frustrated she couldn't get him to answer. She felt so many feelings at once. She was frustrated and confused. It was hard to concentrate on any one thought with him kneeling behind her. She was terrified, yet so confused. Her body was responding to his. She felt the brush of his fingers against her hand as he wrapped the rope around them and it was as if she had just rubbed her feet along her carpet and touched a door knob–shock. Being tied up excited her. Why? It made no rational sense. She needed to get her head in the game. She was unused to her body reacting in any way to a man like she was reacting to this stranger with a gun.

He wanted her underneath him, to feel her body respond to his touch, but he remained closed-lipped. He would never take advantage of a woman. He couldn't. Above all, he respected women, even the ones that were working for the GIA. He would always treat a lady like exactly that, but Emma brought out his basest desires. Desires he had kept hidden. Desires that remained as fantasies to him.

He pulled her chair until her knees were facing his chest. He reached up and tucked a strand of her hair behind her ear, but she jerked her head away from his touch.

He reached for her face again, and again she jerked her head away. *What the fuck was going on?* She would fight these feelings. She would fight with everything she had. She tested her ropes and found they weren't that tight. She might be able to free herself from her bonds. "Who do you work for? Why are you here?" she rambled on in exasperation.

The back of his fingers came close to caress her face again, and this time she felt his touch the whole way to her soul. It was as if his was the first touch she'd ever experienced. She felt her stomach heat. He was still so close to her, his chest against her knees. She could smell his woodsy, musky smell, and it left her confused and overwhelmed.

Did she want him to touch her? Rationally, she couldn't understand this need he created inside her. *This is crazy. This man broke into your home. This man tied you up. This man has a gun pointed at your head.* She shook her head, trying, unsuccessfully, to rid thoughts of him without a shirt from her mind. There was something in his eyes: a goodness. She could see through him like he were made of glass. He didn't mean to hurt her. *Then why does he have a gun pointed at your head?* Her instincts told her that this man was a good man. She was sure that if she could convince him that he had the wrong woman, he would not harm her.

She felt it again, his chest brushing against her knees, sending electricity straight to her core. *Why am I so attracted to him? Why do I know that he will not hurt me? Think. Listen to your mind.*

Her mind was telling her that a strange man was standing in her kitchen after tying her up and held his gun pointed directly at her head. Regardless of her feelings, she had to try something. What if her instincts were wrong?

"Please," she begged, trying a new tactic, "tell me why you are here. Please. What do you want with me?"

He stood and walked to the kitchen door. She took advantage of his lack of attention by working to remove the ropes from her wrists.

"I think you already know the answers to your questions. Perhaps it has something to do with whom *you* are working for these days," he growled as he turned around to face her again. He was pissed such a beautiful creature was out of his reach because she was loyal to the GIA. "If you weren't such a bad person, Emma, we wouldn't be here," he retorted. "Someone is paying me a great deal of money to deliver you to them. Maybe you should be more careful about whom you associate with," he continued as he stared straight into her soul.

Emma wondered what he was talking about. "There must be some mistake," she explained. "I work for the Department of Defense."

"That is not what my sources have confirmed," he said.

He really did admire the view. Her lush lips calling to his cock from across the room. He stared at her lips, and she took notice. How he would love to feel those beautiful lips wrapped around his hard member.

She worked feverishly, but oh so cautiously, to rid her hands of the ropes. He approached her, gun raised, then bent forward and pressed his nose into her neck. *Was he smelling her?*

He backed away, looking regretful. "It's a pity you work for the GIA, Emma. You're a very beautiful woman," he commented as he checked on her bonds, letting his fingers linger on her hand.

The ropes were still in place. Thank God Emma hadn't worked her hands out of them completely yet. She thought about his comments and wondered who the GIA was. He had the wrong person.

Feeling secure in her bondage, Michael walked into her living room to gaze out of her expansive front windows, admiring the thick blanket of snow that covered everything. He always did take time to stop and smell the roses.

Emma didn't waste any time. She worked feverishly removing the remaining bondage. Once free, she quietly made her way to her back door, shoved her feet into her boots, and slipped out of her cabin. She took off running into the forest. It was freezing, big snowflakes were falling all around her, and all she had on was her tank top and pajama bottoms. *She would freeze to death before he could deliver her.* She should have grabbed her keys and made her way to her car.

Michael walked back into the kitchen and noticed the ropes lying on the floor and the back door ajar.

"Fuck," he cried as he reached in his bag and grabbed his flashlight before charging through the back door and into the woods.

Emma had no time to contemplate what to do as the back door swung open and Michael bolted in her direction. She took off running up the hill. She ran and ran as fast as she could, deeper and deeper into the forest. Stumbling a few times, she managed to haul herself back up again. Having hiked these woods numerous times over her years at the cabin, she knew exactly where to go. She stumbled and crawled but eventually made her way to a small cavern opening in the side of the hill.

The snow should make it much easier to track her, Michael thought. He heard a branch break, and he took off running in the direction of the sound. She would freeze out here, and he couldn't allow that. Wearing his heavy North Face jacket, long-sleeve Henley t-shirt, fleece-lined black pants, and winter boots, he was warm enough, but she wasn't wearing anything. He had to find her in the next thirty minutes or frostbite would set in.

Listening for a moment, all he could hear was his heartbeat thumping against his chest. He had to find her. Then he heard her cry as she fell and hit the snow-packed earth. He began moving in that direction. By the time he found her footprints in the snow, she was gone. He followed her prints until they disappeared near a rock formation halfway up the face of the mountain. He walked around slowly, listening and observing. He couldn't hear anything, so he observed every aspect of the rocks that laid around him.

At the bottom of one of the rock formations he noticed a small opening. With his gun drawn, he crawled through the narrow entrance. When he spotted her, he immediately pointed his gun at her chest. She was cowered against the back of the cave, shaking. He approached her as he would a wounded animal. Pointing the flashlight at her, he could see her fingers were already a patchy white. He knew, at that moment, he didn't want her to ever look at him with such fear in her eyes again.

"How are your fingers feeling," he kindly asked her as he approached deliberately.

"They're numb and tingly," she whispered. She was confused again, happy that he found her because she wouldn't last out in the cold but unwilling to go back to being captive. He had spoken to her with such sincerity and her gut, which she never listened to, said he was not a bad person even though he was pointing a gun at her. Such a contradiction.

Her ears were drained white, too. Thinking quickly back upon his training, he realized he had to get her warmed up fast or frostbite and gangrene could set in. She could lose her extremities. First, he removed his coat and wrapped it around her shoulders. Then he dropped his gun, squatted to her sitting position, and brought her hands under his shirt, placing them against his skin. He shivered against her touch.

He placed his hands over hers and pressed her fingers into his tight stomach. His muscles went rigid.

He waited a few minutes until he could feel the cold dissipate a little and said, "We have to get you back to your cabin, or you'll get hypothermia out here."

Emma was too cold to argue. She stood with him, the instinctual part of her body winning out. She was in survival mode. *So much for dying before being delivered.* She would have to think of another way. He brought the gun back up and signaled for her to move in front of him. She complied, and he followed her back to the cabin.

CLOSER

CHAPTER
FOUR

Once inside, he motioned for her to sit down. Placing the gun on the kitchen table, he knelt down in front of her. He removed her right boot and then her left boot, observing her feet were a patchy white as well.

"I am going to run you a warm bath to raise your body temperature," he apologized as he stood. He pulled more rope out of his bag and tied her hands more securely behind her back. He made sure that she couldn't get out of the ropes this time. He couldn't even fit a finger underneath. He turned towards the bathroom, and then stopped and looked back over his shoulder. "Are you going to run again? I'll just track you down. It's what I do, and I'm very good at it." Without waiting for an answer, he removed his gun from the table and advanced to her bathroom.

Like the rest of her house, it was a spacious area. The walls in the bathroom reminded him of a day spa advertisement he had once seen. They were a light olive green, and the floors were made of the same blond hardwood. The Jacuzzi tub was separate from the shower and larger than he expected. In his mind, he could clearly see her luscious body under the warm water soaking the stress away. He could visualize the way the water pebbled on her breasts as it ran down her soft stomach. He started the water, running his hand under it to make sure it was the perfect temperature.

As the water filled the tub, he untied her hands. She walked, teeth chattering and body trembling, into the bathroom as he followed behind. She was determined to get some answers. "To whom do you plan on delivering me?" she demanded. He remained seated on the edge of the tub, hand still under the water. He caught her eye and peered inside her mind. She demanded, "Tell me."

"I'm going to deliver you to an organization which will keep you from helping the GIA," Michael confessed as he shook the water from his hand, the gun resting on his thigh.

"What's the GIA?" she asked, wrapping her arms around her midsection, shivering.

"The GIA is the codename for the Armed Islamic Terrorist group you work for, but I have a feeling you already knew that," he said, disgustedly thinking about how he could never have the beautiful creature who stood courageous and trembling in front of him.

Her eyes widened in horror. "I don't work for the GIA. I work for the Department of Defense," she exclaimed.

The look of shock in her eyes had Michael second-guessing everything he knew about life until that exact moment. He'd always trusted the intel he had been given. Could he have received bad intelligence? Did Rob know? There was no way this woman worked for the GIA. Her look of innocence and panic at the mention of their name told him that much.

Should he tell her everything? His interrogation training told him she was telling the truth. Still, he had valid intel that said she was. It was evident that she didn't know who the GIA was, nor did she work for them. But if that were true, what did it all mean? Who had hired him to kidnap her and why? Why would his best friend provide him with bad intel? He had to talk to Rob or Blackrain Security to get some answers. Someone needed to tell him exactly what the fuck he was doing in this beautiful woman's home. Should he tell her what he was doing there? Should he tell her what the Intel said? Should he dare to hope that he had a chance with her after what he put her through?

He needed to tell her to find out exactly what she knew. Maybe she could lend a clue as to what his real purpose was. Was it to prevent her from divulging state secrets like he'd been led to believe, or was there something else going on here and was he just being used as a means to an end? He didn't like that thought. It meant Rob knew more than he'd told him. But why?

He pulled his cell phone out of his front pocket and dialed Rob's number. It rang several times, but it went to voicemail. "Rob, man. It's me. What the fuck is going on? Emma Welby does not work for the GIA. Call me." He had no choice now. He had to tell her what the Intel said. He had to get to the bottom of this.

"Someone hired me. Told me you worked for the GIA and you had to be stopped. They said you plan on turning over a dangerous new weapon. They are paying me two hundred grand to deliver you. Get undressed," he demanded, pointing the gun at her again, still not sure of what to do. He trusted Rob with his life, yet at the same time, he believed Emma.

She self-consciously removed her tank top. She wasn't wearing a bra.

Michael stared at her like a man starved. He yearned to touch those round, plump breasts. He wanted to taste her. He gazed longingly at her body.

"Can I have some privacy please?" she asked, feeling way too uncomfortable being naked in front of this man. He was looking at her like the Wolf looked at Little Red Riding Hood.

"Remove your pants," he commanded, never moving the gun from the leveled position of her chest. He knew he was now taking advantage of her, but something inside of him had to see her naked.

She hooked her thumbs in her pants and panties and with one move, removed both to the bottom of her feet. She never felt so self-conscious in her life. She brought her arms up to cover her breasts.

At the sight of her naked body, Michael was immediately harder than he had ever remembered feeling in his thirty years on earth. His eyes were drawn from her breasts to the apex of her thighs. All he wanted was to taste her, just once. He instinctively knew she would taste better than anything he had ever experienced.

"Get into the tub and get warm. We have to slowly raise your body temperature or you could get sick," he pleaded as he tore his eyes away from her body.

She did need to get warm and fast. Emma knew the look in his eyes was an earnest one. She could hear the sincerity in his voice. It was that sincerity which confused her more because he looked like a cat playing with a mouse. She felt conflicted. Here was a stranger pointing a gun at her naked body, yet she wasn't afraid. She should be scared, but her instincts said he wasn't going to hurt her— physically anyways. *Should she listen?*

"I'll leave you alone to bathe," he said, walking towards the bathroom door. He pulled the door closed behind him and went to dream about the ways he could make her body respond to his. He sat on her couch, directly facing the bathroom door. He'd seen that the window in the bathroom was a small one high above her Jacuzzi tub. She wouldn't be escaping again.

He fantasized about how wet he could make her when he ran his tongue from the base of her neck to that tender spot where her ear met flesh. He wondered if she would purr if he gently nibbled at the spot where her shoulder met her neck. He wondered how wet she would be as he slid a finger deep into her core. He imagined sucking on that same finger, tasting her sweet juice. Could he keep these urges under control?

The bath gave Emma the perfect opportunity to think. Someone wanted her, no doubt for the knowledge she could provide on Project Hummingbird. She already knew there was a black market for this weapon, but she had always felt safe enough in the knowledge that not many people had known of her project. Someone must be selling out, someone high up in the chain of command. That was the only way anyone could possibly know about her work. But who?

In truth, there were only a handful of people that knew of the project, all with the highest level security clearance that one could achieve. Was it someone at the DOD or the CIA? Who would betray their country like that? She had no way of knowing and no way to find out. He planned on delivering her to a group who would keep her from divulging her secrets to the GIA. That just didn't make sense. She had Top Secret clearance, which meant the government trusted her not to consort with anyone. This had to be the work of a terrorist group, possibly even the same group Michael thought he was helping to protect the United States against. What would they do with her? Would they torture or rape her because she wouldn't give up what she knew easily?

She knew she would die as soon as they had the information they needed from her. Although she had never heard their code name, GIA, before, she knew The Armed Islamic Group was no joke. They were based in Algeria and were ruthless kidnappers and terrorists. Now, it appeared, a cell was here in the United States. Was their target also here? Once they had her knowledge, once they knew how to build a Hummingbird, it was only a matter of time before they flew it into the capital and took out the President of the United States and all of his security detail. They could walk in and take the President. They'd have the leverage to achieve anything they wanted. Surely the United States didn't negotiate with terrorists, but what would happen if they somehow got the President, or worse, his family?

Her stress only increased with her body temperature. She had to find a way out of this mess. Maybe she could convince Michael. He seemed sincere in his concern for her. She knew from the way he devoured her with his eyes, he wanted her. Maybe she could play him.

Who was she kidding? She wasn't a sex kitten like Bethany. She didn't know how to use her feminine wiles to seduce a man. She wouldn't even know what seducing a man looked like. Maybe she could arouse sympathy in him and bring him around to her cause.

Should she tell him what she was working on? It was her greatest secret and her life's work. If she took a chance and told him, he could use it against her. She could lose her reputation and her job. She worked so hard to achieve everything she had. She spent her whole life working towards this one goal. Could she tell him? Would it work? Once he knew the truth, perhaps he would change his mind.

However, he was attempting to kidnap her. He did have a gun that he'd kept on her. He had used his gun to order her to get undressed. What kind of man did that? If he was truly kidnapping her out of fear for his country, maybe she could use that fear. That would require divulging state secrets, but if it achieved her objective, then she was willing, because as it stood now, she would most likely be tortured and raped once she was handed over to the GIA. And she had no idea how long she could hold out. She wasn't trained to withstand torture. What she had to decide now was which was more important, her project or her life?

She reappeared with a bathrobe wrapped snuggly around her body. She knew that telling him the truth was the only way to gain his trust. And in gaining his trust, he would believe her and not hand her over to the GIA or whoever was trying to kidnap her. "I think there are some things you need to know," she conceded as she walked into the living room.

She hoped this plan of bringing him to her side would work. After all, he said he was "hired" and he definitely gave off a military vibe. He had to be a patriot if he thought he was doing the right thing by delivering her to the people who would keep her from spilling her secrets to the GIA.

Michael mentally undressed her as she reemerged from the bathroom. Now that he knew what was underneath the clothing, he could only picture her naked in his mind. Their eyes met, and he exposed the desire and insecurity he felt where she was concerned.

As Emma peered into his caramel brown orbs, she felt that none-too-familiar heat in her belly. She was definitely attracted to this man, but she imagined most women would be. And his eyes . . . his light caramel colored eyes made her want to confess her darkest fantasies to him. She imagined her hands twisting in his curls as she pulled his head tighter against her body. He was a good six inches taller than she was. Where she was all soft, he was hard and muscular. *Just great, now she was attracted to her abductor. But how could she even trust this man?*

She'd never before trusted her gut. Her head was giving her a hell of a hard time. She had always relied strictly on her intellect. She'd never needed to use her intuition over her rational thought, but, if she was going to win him over, she needed to trust her feelings now. Her gut screamed at her to trust him, but her head said don't. Once he knew the truth, he would protect her. She felt it. She was sure of it. She quieted her mind and listened to her feelings. *Here goes nothing.*

He stalked her like a hyena approaches a gazelle. He drew closer until they were a breath apart. He was going to kiss her. Her head got all swimmy, something that never had happened to her before. She felt dizzy, like her legs were going to give out. And then she felt it, his hot mouth closed over her tightly drawn lips. Still in her head, she fought it, she pulled back and slapped his face, forcing his head to the side.

Michael touched his cheek, rubbing the spot she slapped. Everything about her pulled him to her. He was the proverbial moth to the flame.

He looked into her eyes and smiled. She was a tough one. He didn't mind the chase, but he knew without a doubt after tasting her, he would have her willingly give herself to him.

He spoke calmly, apologetically, his eyes fixated upon hers. He didn't know what had come over him other than he had to touch her. "Why don't I fix you a cup of tea?" he asked as he allowed her to walk away from his hard body.

"I would love a cup, thank you," she retorted, still shocked he had kissed her and even more so because she had liked it.

He padded into her kitchen and she followed. "Where do you keep your tea?" he asked, opening cabinet after cabinet until she responded.

"That one." She pointed.

He reached inside and pulled out the teabags, setting them on the counter. He grabbed the kettle from the stove and filled it with water. She sat down on the stool at the breakfast bar facing the kitchen. She couldn't help but notice how very much at home he looked in her space, even with the gun in his hand.

It was now or never, but she was torn. Her head said not to trust him. But this time she was going to have to listen to her gut. This was her only plan, and if it worked, he could help her, she just knew it.

"I work for the DOD on a top secret project. Only a handful of people know of it," she confessed. "I'm the only engineer currently working on a robotic prototype. It will be completed and fully operational in three weeks. Once it's complete, it will be able to fly, undetected, into any terrorist group in the world and release a pharmacological weapon—a powerful anesthetic and sedative chemical compound that degrades the functioning of the brain and renders the subject incapacitated for eight hours. In theory, that is enough time for the military to move in and clean up the cell. There is, however, a black market for this type of technology. If this technology fell into terrorists' hands, not only would they have a new weapon, but they would have a delivery system for all of the biochemical weapons that are currently against the Biological and Toxin Weapons Convention.

"Terrorists could mist targets with Sarin, mustard gas, cyanide, phosgene, or any other number of agents causing incapacitation or death." She sighed audibly when she finished speaking, accepting the tea Michael handed her. "I'm the only one with the knowledge of a working delivery system. I can see why someone wants what I know," she continued.

"Are you working for a terrorist organization?" he asked.

"No, I don't work for a terrorist organization," she professed.

"Then the people I'm working for aren't people who want to keep you from divulging state secrets to terrorists?" he questioned, a spark of recognition in his eyes.

Michael did believe her with all of his heart. There was no way this beautiful, intelligent, courageous woman was working against the very country she pledged to be protecting with her new weapon.

He believed her, and it wasn't just because he wanted to pervert her. He believed her because she was worthy of a top secret security clearance. He knew what he had to go through to get that level of clearance. One's whole life was evaluated and inspected until the government found sufficient proof of trustworthiness. Credit checks were run, college classmates were contacted, and siblings were investigated. He believed her because her eyes communicated what words never could: *truth.*

But this left Michael in a precarious position. He trusted Rob. Why would Rob set him up in anything that wasn't above board? He would wait until his employer called and make his plan then. He was, however, certain about one thing: he wouldn't be delivering Emma anywhere but to her bed.

He walked around to stand beside her, gun still in his right hand. He placed his gun on the counter and took the hand holding her tea cup, lowering it to the counter. Spinning her around on the stool, he spread her knees with his leg. He stepped between her legs, coming closer to her lips. Instead of kissing her, he placed his big arms around her rather petite body and hugged her.

He whispered in her ear a sincere promise, "I will protect you."

Emma felt goose bumps rise along the edges of her skin. She sat there, and for some strange reason, allowed Michael to hug her. Maybe it was because he believed her. Maybe she was able to convince him he was working for the wrong side. Whatever the reason, it felt good—too good—to be held by him. He was, after all, the direct conduit between her and the men who wanted her.

As they stood in the kitchen, Michael could never remember a time when a woman felt so good, so right, pressed against him. He felt her soft breasts mold against his hard chest. He pulled her closer, her arms still hanging at her sides.

He wasn't a bad looking man and knew women found him attractive, but he wondered about her, because Emma felt completely different in his arms. The thought of losing her plagued his mind. Now, the hard part would be convincing her to trust him. He knew she only told him what was necessary to convince him to help her. He could feel her seriousness coming off her like a palpable energy. She had won. She had used her intelligence and the truth to convince him what he was doing was wrong, that she was the one needed protecting.

"Are you in the military?" she asked.

"Yes, a Green Beret," he responded matter-of-factly.

"How long did you serve?" she asked as her eyes connected with his to gauge the truth of his statements.

"Eight years with the Army," he replied honestly, holding the eye contact.

He hadn't lied to her yet and he wasn't going to start now. He ran his hands up and down the sides of her arms, reassuring her that she could trust him. He would be there for her.

She stood to go get dressed, pushing Michael out of her space. He reluctantly let her go.

When she returned to the living room, Michael was building a fire. She was dressed in a warm cowl-neck sweater and jeans with a hole in the knee. Her feet were bare.

"It's going to be a long night," Michael mumbled to himself after he saw how sexy she looked. "Are you hungry? I could use something to eat," Michael confessed.

"Sure, I can make us some sandwiches and chips." She stood and went to the kitchen. He didn't follow, choosing instead to enjoy the fire. A few moments later, she reemerged from the kitchen with two plates. She set the plates on the coffee table and went back to get their drinks.

"Is water okay?" she shouted from the kitchen.

"Do you have any milk?" he asked.

"Sure." She came back into the living room with a glass of water for herself and a tall glass of milk for Michael. She set the drinks next to the plates. Michael picked up his plate and quickly ate his sandwich. Emma took delicate, small bites. Michael was done with his before Emma had finished half of hers. "Do you want me to make you another?"

"Please. I haven't eaten much today." Emma went to make him another sandwich. He ate the second with the same enthusiasm with which he ate the first.

When their stomachs were full, dirty plates and glasses on the coffee table, Michael gathered the dishes and took them to the kitchen sink. Emma followed and watched as Michael rinsed their plates and glasses and placed them into the dishwasher.

Back in the living room, Emma wondered aloud, "What's the plan?"

He sat down on the red couch and patted the seat next to him. His plans were to have her lying naked beneath him.

She sat down, their shoulders accidentally touching. The electricity that sparked between them was palpable. His touch went straight to her core. She felt her face flush. She cast her eyes towards her lap and stared at her twisting hands. His voice pulled her eyes up. They connected with his as he spoke.

"I'm going to wait until my employer calls me before I make a plan. I need the information he's going to provide before I can figure out a way to keep you safe. But until he calls, we probably should get some sleep," he said, watching her eyes sparkle in the firelight.

Emma watched as Michael stood and separated the logs, taking care to securely close the glass pane. She noticed that he made sure to leave the damper open so the fire would die out naturally. She rose from the couch and noticed his gun was now lying on the end table. She knew, at that moment, he was on her side. Her head told her to grab the gun and flee, but her body was paralyzed. What was going on? Why did her heart trust Michael so completely? She made her way to the stairs, and he followed.

Michael wanted her in a way he hadn't ever felt before. Something inside him craved her touch, which is why he left his gun sitting on the table. He would never leave his gun.

"I am going to sleep in here tonight, in that chair," he said, pointing to the chaise lounge in the corner of her loft bedroom.

"Why? I'm not going anywhere," she confessed as she grabbed her night clothes from the dresser and made her way to the bathroom.

He really hoped she dressed in something unattractive, something that hid her curves from his mind, or he might be crawling into bed with her.

She earned a huge smile when she stepped out of the bathroom. "You look adorable," Michael said before he realized what he was saying.

"Thank you?" she said uncertainly.

She stood in a pair of sweatpants covered in splotches of paint and t-shirt that reached her knees. His hand found the button on his jeans and he undid them. She watched unapologetically as he removed his pants. He supposed that if he could watch her, she most certainly had the right to watch him. He folded his jeans and tossed them onto the ottoman in front of the chaise lounge. She tossed a blanket in his direction. He caught it and sat down as if getting comfortable for the night. He knew he would never sleep, not with her so close. He would agonize all night about wanting something he couldn't have.

She crawled into bed, pulling the covers up to her neck. "Thank you," she said.

"For what?" he asked, looking at her in the moonlight.

"For believing me. For not handing me over to the bad guys. For saying you will protect me," she rambled on, feeling foolish for thanking the man who had planned on kidnapping her.

He didn't respond. Instead, his feelings stirred within his core. So he sat on the lounge chair in the corner of her loft with only his thoughts to keep him warm. Tonight he would watch over her while she slept.

It wasn't long before Michael heard the deep, even breathing coming from Emma. She was sleeping soundly in her king size bed. Michael watched over her like he promised, although he had a killer hard-on from the thoughts that were whirling through his mind.

It wasn't long before he heard her moan. Was it a pleasure filled moan or a moan filled with anguish over what he had put her through today? That thought threw a splash of cold water on his raging member. She tossed and turned, and he wondered what she was dreaming about.

Michael spread her legs with his hands, pushing her open to accept his tongue. He dragged his rough fingers up the hypersensitive flesh of her calf, following

his hand with a trail of kisses. He stopped at her center and spread her folds with his thick fingers. He dipped his head, lapping at her clit. He circled her with a pressured tongue. She arched under his touch, pushing her core closer to his mouth. Her hand finally found its way into his curls, firmly entangled in his hair, and forced his head closer.

Michael continued lapping at her clit and then dipped his tongue, pushing it into her core. He licked and sucked at the entrance of her body. Then, as he resumed licking her clit with pressured, rhythmic strokes, he pushed at her opening with two fingers. His fingers slid easily inside her. He slowly moved his fingers in and out of her slick, hot center as he suckled on her clit.

He was licking furiously up and down and around her nub applying the perfect amount of pressure while her hand pulled him roughly, closer to her. She held his hair to bring his mouth where she needed it while she arched her hips, moving them back and forth against his mouth. His hand made its way up her belly to her bare breasts and pinched her nipple.

He continued sliding his fingers in and out of her body, sucking and licking her clit, pushing her closer and closer to the edge.

She lifted her back off of the bed and cried out, "Michael."

Her spoken word woke her up. She felt herself coming down from her intense orgasm. What had she just done? God, she prayed he was asleep. He couldn't know she was attracted to him. Not to the extent that it had her dreaming about his tongue on her body. She peered over at his sleeping form in the chair. Thank God, she thought as she finally came down for her orgasm.

What did this mean, dreaming about Michael the way she had? Was it the adrenaline that caused her to masturbate in her sleep, something which had never happened before? She hardly ever reached orgasm when she had sex with a man because she was always stuck in her head, thinking about what he was thinking, always drawing upon the worst case scenario: *Sure he's sleeping with you, but it is only because he wants the release.* She really had to work on her body image. Intellectually, she knew she was attractive, but she never felt that guys found her that attractive, even though they told her they did. She had serious issues. With Michael, that wasn't the case. She knew, body and soul, he was attracted to her. He said it with the way he destroyed her with his eyes.

Did she really want Michael that badly? She was attracted to him, which was now painfully obvious, and she believed he was attracted to her. But it had to be the situation. She had never felt these intense feelings before. She had to figure out what they meant before she did something her head would regret.

She lay there painfully awake. All she could hear was her own heavy breath escaping her mouth. She listened carefully for Michael's slow, easy breaths. She longed to be nestled safely in his arms, but he was all the way across the room in that damn chair.

Why didn't she just ask him to sleep with her? What would he think of her if she did? What did that make her, asking her kidnapper to sleep with her? But he was more than that now. He was her protector. At least that is what he promised to be. They could surely sleep in the same bed without touching each other. Although, God knew, she wanted to touch him, affect him, the way he affected her. She wished to touch the very soul of his being. Her dream and subsequent orgasm left her feeling bereft. She craved Michael's touch. She had never experienced anything like it before, and she was certain she probably would never experience anything like it again. After what seemed to be the longest twenty minutes of her life, she whispered his name. Still asleep.

Michael had watched in the moonlight as her hand traveled down her stomach to her center. He saw her hand rubbing herself underneath the covers. God, he prayed, hoping she was dreaming of him. Her free hand had palmed her breast and tugged at the nipple. He'd watched as she arched under the covers, rubbing herself. Michael heard her moans increasing. He could see her hand working harder under the blanket. He had a front row seat to see her pleasuring herself. God, she'd better be dreaming about him.

He would never let her know he had witnessed one of the most erotic sights of his life, a sight that had made him damn near close to coming in his underwear.

He saw her body, although covered, move and arch under the blankets. He heard his name escape her mouth as she found her release.

CLOSER

CHAPTER
SIX

Without curtains, sunlight blasted into the room, a problem Michael thought needed to be addressed. He squinted at the bright light reflecting off the snow. The sight was really awe-inspiring—tree branches layered with two inches of snow. The mountains held a magical quality, which soothed his mind.

Emma was in the same spot he'd left her last night. His morning erection was pressing hard against his boxer briefs. It was a good thing he remained covered.

It hit him then. He'd actually slept all night without booze. What this woman could do for him! She was the balm to his blistering burn. He felt calm in her presence. He had slept through the night with her orgasm fresh on his mind. This was the first good night's rest he'd had since his college days. He needed her. There were no longer any doubts. She was his angel. She was his cure. Now, he just had to make her see it, too.

"Time to get up, sleepy head," he said.

She smiled. "I thought it was all just a dream," she confessed.

"What? That someone wants to kidnap you?" he retorted.

"No. That you were here," she whispered.

He was definitely making progress. "I am here, Emma. You better get used to it."

Her eyes met his, and they held each other's gaze for what felt like the briefest of seconds. It wasn't awkward like she thought it was going to be. He was still here. He still wanted to protect her.

She got out of bed. God, after the night she had, she must look a wreck. She had to rectify the situation. She shuffled her way into the bathroom telling Michael she was going to take a shower.

Michael watched the door close. Great, now he got to imagine the way the water pebbled and beaded down her body. He wanted to lick the water from her bare breasts. He was hard again just thinking about her. She was no ordinary woman. He would have been able to resist an ordinary woman. He hungered for Emma, for her touch, her taste, her moans.

Emma exited the shower dressed in her robe. She ran a brush through her hair, which lay loosely around her shoulders. She put her glasses on and brushed her teeth.

She found Michael in the kitchen pouring two cups of coffee. "What do you take in your coffee?" he asked her, opening the fridge to get out the milk for his cup.

"Cream and sugar please," she responded shyly. Why was she feeling shy around him all of a sudden?

He fixed her coffee and handed it to her across the kitchen bar where she sat on the same stool she'd sat on the night before. He came to her side, turning her around so she was facing him.

Just like last night, he leaned in-between her legs, but this time he took her mouth in a possessive kiss, which had her parting her lips to allow him access. She didn't know where this "trusting her gut" would take her, but she sure was enjoying the feel of being his, even if it was just for the moment.

Michael pulled back from the kiss to admire the sight before him. With her hair dried and wavy against her shoulders, her glasses perched at the bottom of her nose, her robe open in the front, revealing perfectly large breasts, he couldn't help himself. He found his hand tracing the edges of her robe, dipping his calloused fingers lower onto the swell of her bosom. He lightly fingered her breasts. A moan escaped her lips, and his erection pushed harder against his pants, straining the zipper until he was afraid it would bust. He pushed further into her, recapturing her mouth. This time his kiss was demanding.

She gave as good as she got, kissing him back, equally fervent. Her hands wandered their way under his shirt to trace the outline of his rock-hard abs. *Was this really happening?* She ran her hands under his shirt up to his chest. This time it was he who moaned at the contact. He pulled her to the edge of her seat and pushed up against her center. She could feel his attraction through his pants pressed against her body.

He picked her up like a petite thing and placed her on the kitchen table, letting her robe fall open.

A Renoir, that's what she looked like—a fine work of art. She was a masterpiece made just for him, her hips and stomach soft to his calloused touch. Running the tips of his fingers over her body, he stroked up and down her thighs, paying careful attention to her hips. How he loved her hips.

Emma moved to the kitchen table and laid before him. She was aching at her very center. Her body wanted him. She wanted him. She wasn't going to deny her feelings any longer, regardless of what was causing them.

He grabbed her hips and pulled her closer to the edge of the kitchen table.

"Lose the shirt," she demanded. He complied, tearing the shirt over his head to stand in front of her in all of his sex-god goodness. She ran her eyes over his perfectly formed six-pack abs and followed the V which led to his holy land—a land she would surely worship.

Michael leaned over and kissed her ever so reverently, paying homage to her body, to her being. He placed open-mouth kisses along her jawline, moving down to her breasts. He suckled her pert nipple, pressing it against the roof of his mouth with his tongue. A moan escaped her lips as she arched into his touch. He was falling for this smart, courageous, woman. Her earth scent mixed with his musky scent to form an aroma uniquely their own.

He could hear his heart beat in his ears as she lay bare before him, and he still had on his pants. He would remedy that problem really quickly. He left her lying on top of the kitchen table, her body bared to him as he pulled away. This time he turned slightly around and bent to remove his boots. He threw his pants onto the growing pile of clothes. He was just about to remove his boxer briefs when his cell phone rang. He contemplated not answering. However, as it was probably information he needed to formulate a plan to protect her, he had to get it. If he did his job, and if he kept her safe, he could have her to himself later. He bent down and kissed her hard and quick. Then he went to dig into his pants pocket for his phone.

Pulling it out, he spoke curtly. "Yeah?" as he walked into the living room.

She sat up suddenly, again feeling deprived, the way she felt after coming last night. How had she come to like him so much, under the circumstances, in so little time? Clearly her head was not in the game. She realized she was led solely by her body. She got off the table and readjusted her robe. She tightly tied the belt around her waist and sat back down at the bar stool. She poured her and Michael a fresh cup of coffee.

Michael reentered the room in just his boxer briefs, grabbed his pile of clothing, and started dressing.

She watched under hooded eyes. Truth be told, she was still wet from the earlier contact. She really should get dressed herself. She made her way off the bar stool and began to walk past him into the living room to reach the stairs. He grabbed her by the arm and turned her around to face him.

"Where are you going?" he asked, pulling her closer to him.

"I'm going to get dressed. I've been in this robe long enough," she responded.

"Just so you know," he whispered, his breath on her lips, "we are nowhere near finished."

She shivered at his promise.

She returned to the living room in a new pair of jeans and a turtleneck sweater, one that hugged all the curves of her body. She sat next to Michael on the couch.

"That was my employer, the real kidnapper. His name is Ahmed El-Amin, and he has a heavy Algerian accent, so I can only conclude he works for the GIA." Michael continued, "I am to drop you off at a warehouse in Pittsburgh. I told him it's a two-day drive from here. He said he'd be there waiting for your arrival. I plan to make the drop."

She looked up at him with a sadness that touched his heart.

"I'm not leaving you with him for God's sake," he admonished. "When we get there, I'll take him instead. Then I'll interrogate him for information about his cell."

"You really think you can get him to tell you that type of information? I thought they were all martyrs willing to die for their cause."

"Who said anything about killing him? I'll just make him wish he were dead." He choked on the laugh which escaped his throat.

She wondered why he would take such pleasure in hurting another person. "What could possibly be so funny?" she asked.

"I have a plan. I know exactly what I am going to do to the man who wants to take you from me," he said.

Did she just hear him right? Take her from him?

"I'm going to protect you," he continued. "After we get the information we need, I'll make a few phone calls to Homeland Security, and they can stop this cell in its tracks.

A logical plan, one her brain could follow, Emma thought. She liked that.

"Go. Pack a bag. We'll be gone a week max. Pack as light as you can. One bag, okay?" he asked.

She started to go do as he bid, but before she could, he pulled her back down to him and moved his face quickly into hers.

His lips were a hair's breath away from hers when he whispered, "I promise on my life, nothing will happen to you. I need you to trust me. Do you trust me?

She looked into his eyes and without a moment's thought replied, "Yes."

He kissed her again tenderly. Taking his hand and wrapping it roughly in the back of her hair to tilt her face against his, he pulled her closer. With her lips parted, he took advantage and continued his exploration of her mouth. Their tongues met and danced a lover's dance. They were both breathing heavy. She could feel her heartbeat pounding out a rhythm against her chest. She wrapped her hands around his neck and, although it was hardly possible, pulled him closer to her. Picking her up, he placed her on his lap. She smiled through their kiss. She would never grow tired of him tossing her around like she was light as a feather. She could feel how much he wanted her against her derriere.

Relinquishing her hair, he grabbed hold of her hips, rocking them back and forth over his cock to try and get some satisfaction. How long could he wait to have her? She seemed willing enough. Still, he did not want to rush her. Well, yes he did, he thought, but he wasn't going to. After all, they both had a two-day drive ahead of them. He hesitantly pulled back, taking care to grind her hips into his bulging cock once more for good measure. If he didn't stop now, he wasn't going to.

She stood up and reached out her hand. Placing his hand in hers and following her upstairs to the bedroom was hard for him because he knew he would not get any relief from his erection that was dripping with pre-cum.

In the top of her closet, Emma found her duffle bag, which she began filling with essentials. It was a good thing she never wore makeup, she thought as she exited the bathroom with her toiletries.

Michael sat, watching, on the corner of her unmade bed. Her limbs moved like a graceful ballet dancer and that enthralled him. Once again, he found himself imagining her body under his, responding to his ministrations. The smell of lavender filled the room. It smelled like her. As if in a tense wartime situation, he had to take several deep breaths, holding them in the pit of his stomach before releasing his pent-up frustration into the air, effectively calming his mind. They had to get on the road.

After she had finished packing her bag, a groan escaped her lips. She tried to quickly cover it with a cough, but it was too late, Michael heard her.

"What's wrong, Emma?" he asked.

How could she answer that question? She didn't want to leave the safety of her home when he was in it. She wanted him naked, on top of her. She didn't want to drive two days to meet a terrorist. She didn't want to talk to Homeland Security and risk jeopardizing her project that basically defined who she was. Her project meant everything to her. To risk it was unacceptable. Maybe it was just the situation, but he was mentally stimulating her with his quick mind and his plan of action, and she was chemically attracted to him. She burned with longing to feel his hands on her bare body. Mostly, she didn't want to leave his presence. After this was over, he would leave. Sure they would have sex, but he would leave and go back to his life before her. She couldn't let her heart get involved. She needed to remain in her head.

Determined, she got up. She put on pink socks and her brown Ugg boots. She stepped into the bathroom and pulled her hair back into a loose chignon, pieces falling, framing her face. Squeezing toothpaste onto her toothbrush, she quickly brushed her teeth.

She walked back into the bedroom and was once again met by his grin that spread ear to ear. She admired the way he looked in his long-sleeve Henley t-shirt and the way the shirt showed off the muscles in his back, forming that damn V.

In the living room, he retrieved his boots. He carried them into her breakfast nook and sat at the table.

"Do we have time for one more cup of coffee? I usually drink two before I start my day," she asked as she refilled the mugs from earlier.

"We don't have much time," he said as he stood.

Walking over to him, her arm outstretched, she handed him a cup, remembering to add the cream just the way he liked it. He took it with a smile and a wink. She blushed. *This was just silly. She was being silly. She had to get a grip on her emotions.* They drank their coffee, smiling at each other to pass the time. Walking over to her, he grabbed her coffee mug and placed both mugs in the sink. Then he turned the coffee pot off.

"We need to get going," he said as he picked up his bag.

She put her coat on and buttoned it up. "I'm ready," she responded. They had to get this over with so they both could get back to their lives.

"We'll take my Jeep. It's parked at the bottom of the hill. You wait here while I go get it," he commanded as she sat his bag back on the floor. Not more than five minutes later he was walking back into her house and reaching for her bag.

"I can get it," she huffed at him, trying to take the bag back from his grasp.

"Don't even think about it, pretty lady. My mama raised a gentleman." He winked and went out the door.

She took one look around her house, consciously aware things may go wrong and she may never see her cabin again. She closed the door and locked it up nice and tight. Walking over to the Jeep, she was greeted with his smile.

"Aren't you nervous?" she asked as she climbed in the front seat and pulled the door shut.

He put the car in reverse to turn around and answered, "Nope. This is what I do. And I was trained by and worked with the best." He was pretty sure of himself. Of course, that was something she admired about him, his sexy confidence.

"What exactly did you do for the Army?"

"I can't tell you a lot of what I did, as I am sure you can understand. Classified."

A nagging feeling annoyed her. She wanted him to open up to her the way she had opened up to him. "I told you what it is that I do, and that is highly classified information," she argued, biting on her thumbnail.

She placed her hands in her lap, twisting her fingers until they were white. Here she was divulging state secrets and he couldn't come clean about his past work. Her face reddened, and she bit into the cuticle of her thumb.

"What's wrong, Emma?"

"I basically told you everything about my work, which I was never to tell to another living soul, and you can't tell me about what you did in the past?" she spouted as she shot him a look of frustration.

"Don't get upset. What is it that you want to know?" he asked.

"The basics would be nice," she retorted.

"I was a Special Forces Engineer Sergeant. Basically, I was responsible for blowing stuff up. Anything that had to do with explosives, I was the guy." The color of her face was returning to normal, and she'd stopped biting her cuticle.

He continued, "I was cross trained with the Medic Sergeant, my good friend Rob."

"Did you ever have to save anybody's life?" she asked.

"I didn't do the saving. I just patched up a few guys until they could be saved," he told her, remembering how he couldn't save his brother Leroy. His eyes watered, and he fought at the threatening tears. A lump formed in the back of his throat, and he needed a minute to regain his composure.

"Did you do anything else besides blow things up and stop the bleeding?" she questioned.

He swallowed hard and then casually said, "Well, usually we trained troops in foreign lands in the ways of war, but we also had our own missions like hostage retrieval, reconnaissance, unconventional warfare, counter terrorism, that kind of thing.

"And how long did you spend in the military again?"

"I was in for eight years. I joined right after I graduated with my Bachelors in Political Science, when I was twenty-two."

"How old are you?" she wondered, keeping her eyes on the road in front of them. She knew she was pressing her luck by asking so many questions.

Playing twenty questions with her wasn't getting old. He found he liked being interrogated by her. "Thirty, as of last June," he smiled. "Why? How old are you?" he asked as he looked at her.

"I'm twenty-eight, also as of last June." She returned his smile.

Depressing the knob for the radio, he turned it on and quickly found "Lips of an Angel" by Hinder, effectively ending her interrogation. He allowed the station to play until it faded out. Then he tuned the radio to find another contemporary rock station, which was playing "Alone Together" by Fall Out Boy. That was his favorite song, and he had watched "The Young Blood Chronicles" music videos, parts one through eleven, over and over again.

They drove on in enjoyable silence, listening to bands like Linkin Park and The Killers. She was most surprised when he stopped scanning the stations at Adele's "Make You Feel My Love." He kept peeking at her during Adele's song, and it was making her feel awkward. The song talked about love—an emotion she was not familiar with at all. She spent so much time in her head, she never allowed herself to feel. Could she have feelings for Michael? She wanted him, but was that a feeling? She had heard those stories about love at first sight, but her head didn't believe in such nonsense.

They'd been driving for three hours when he sat up and took notice of a car following close behind them. His erect posture alerted her to danger. He started driving more aggressively, weaving in and out of traffic. She looked behind her and spotted an SUV trying to keep up with them. "What's going on?" she asked breathlessly as she gripped the grab handle above her head.

"Hang on tight. We're being followed. I'm gonna try and lose 'em," he explained.

She sat up straighter herself, turning to stare behind them. All of a sudden, the driver's side mirror exploded. "They're shooting at us!" she screamed.

"Calm down. I will get us out of this," he chided. If ever there was a time he needed her to trust him, it was now. He couldn't be worried about her and this clown chasing them at the same time. "Just close your eyes," he suggested as he overtook a Toyota and squeezed between two cars.

She couldn't. The man was still on their tail and was gaining speed. Michael took the next exit off of I-95 onto a two-lane road. The man kept up and took the same exit. "Damn it!" he exclaimed.

The SUV behind them started shooting again. This time Michael had to swerve or the bullet would have busted the rear window. "Turn off the music. I need to concentrate," he demanded. She complied and pressed the button. Michael sped away into a small town and turned down the first alley he came to. The

SUV followed. Michael wasn't giving the car behind them any time to fire shots. He banked hard to the right and ended up on the road headed out of town. He made another quick left onto a back country road. Just when she thought they had lost the SUV, here it came again, even faster.

"Whoever this fucker is, he's trained," Michael commented as he barreled, white-knuckled, down the road.

The SUV plowed into the right-hand corner of the Jeep, causing Michael to swerve in order to keep the car on the road. The SUV rammed them again, same spot, but this time Michael lost control of the Jeep and crashed it head-on into a tree.

Michael wasted no time going for his gun. He had it out of its holster before she could even lift her head. "Stay down," he commanded.

She tried to tuck her head between her knees and curl up into a tight ball, but the airbags were in her way.

Thank God for airbags, she thought.

Michael took out his knife from his hip holster and slit the airbags, causing them to deflate. Just then her door jerked open and a man appeared. He reached in and began pulling at her arm, but she was still safely belted into the seat. Michael raised his gun and pointed it directly at the man's face. "Let her go," Michael growled.

The man raised his gun and pointed it at her head. "I suggest she come with me, or I will just have to kill her here. You don't really want to see that, do you?" he asked Michael as he reached in and undid her seatbelt. Michael kept his gun pointed at the man's head.

"Drop your weapon or I will shoot her," the man demanded.

Please drop your weapon, Michael. She didn't want to be shot right now or ever for that matter. She knew once the man took her, Michael would find her. She knew Michael wouldn't give up on her.

Michael couldn't risk losing her. But if this bastard took her, how would he get her back? His car was totaled. He couldn't follow them. He was at least five miles from the nearest town.

"Drop it," the man mocked.

Michael found himself laying down his weapon. He got out of his Jeep and walked to the other side to see the man forcing Emma into the passenger side of the SUV. Michael mentally catalogued everything he could about the situation. The kidnapper was American. He could tell by his lack of accent and his three-piece designer suit. Who would be after Emma besides the GIA?

He forced himself to think. The CIA could be out for information. Weren't they always? That would explain the expensive suit and shoes and the standard issued GMC Terrain SUV Emma was currently being belted in to. Still, why would the CIA want her dead? She worked for the DOD. They had to know that. If he was going to go after Emma, he couldn't call the CIA. They would tie him up in paperwork for the next year, not to mention the circumstances under which he and

Emma had met. No, Michael would need his own particular brand of help.

Emma stared at him as the car slowly pulled away from the crash site. Michael mouthed, "I'm coming for you. Stay safe." When she left, she took his breath with him. He realized he had failed to protect her.

He made a mental note of the license plate, definitely government issued: U.S. Government DC2368. The man that had taken Emma no longer worked undercover, that much was clear from his plate. Someone high up the chain of the CIA wanted her. But why? What kind of information did they want? Maybe they wanted her to lead them to the GIA, but he was the only one who knew about his security firm's job to kidnap her. Only he and Rob, he thought in disgust. He had to talk to Rob. That was his first step in finding his breath again.

CLOSER

CIA Special Agent Daniel Ingrams had handcuffed her to the door. What did he think she was going to do, jump out of a speeding vehicle? She stared at him, observing his clean-shaven face and pathetic comb-over. He was an unattractive man with high cheekbones, a large nose, and skinny lips. She would be surprised if he was married. He gave off a "don't touch me" vibe loud and clear.

"What do you want with me?" she asked as she tried to find a comfortable position. She had a hard time turning her body to face his. She managed to turn her head so she could gauge his reactions to her questions.

"What do you think I am going to do with you?" he retorted.

"I work for the Department of Defense. They won't take kindly to me being 'taken,'" she explained as she eyed his profile.

His hands were steady on the wheel. This was a man on a mission. "I know exactly what you do for the DOD. You let me worry about them. You just worry about how to keep yourself alive for the next three days," he censured as he stared ahead at the road in front of him.

"What did I do to you? Why do you want me dead?" she pleaded.

"It's not what you did to me. It's what you know that is going to get you killed. And I am just the man for the job. It's better I kill you to keep what you know out of the hands of the terrorists than you confess state secrets to the GIA," he blurted.

Daniel would be a hero for his actions. His boss would see the error of his ways in closing the case on the Armed Islamic Group before he had a chance to fully vet it. It was true, he worked on the case for over three years and in that time not one message of chatter indicated a threat to any American target. All of it indicated threats against Algerian targets. Still, he wasn't finished. He had made it his personal mission to bring down the GIA after they had taken and killed his best friend who worked as a contractor in Algeria.

Once the CIA closed the case eight months ago, he took it upon himself to continue investigating. And it was a good thing he did, too, or he would not have found out about Emma Welby and her prototype for chemical weapon disbursement. Too bad he couldn't go to his boss with what he had found. The first time he tried, he got his ass chewed out for still investigating in the first place. A much lower level agent was put in charge of the GIA and its subsequent chatter. That agent would deem what was a worthy threat. His boss had said Ingrams had taken things too personally. He needed someone with objectivity, and Ingrams had lost his.

Lost his objectivity. Ingrams would show him. He would neutralize the threat no one else at the Agency seemed concerned about. Still, Ingrams knew. He knew what the GIA wanted, and they weren't going to get it. He would kill Emma first.

"Where are we going?" asked Emma, swallowing the bile that rose in the back of her throat.

"We're taking a little ride to a cabin I rented in Wells. It is part of the Rachel Carson National Wildlife Refuge. It really is quite beautiful as the property is adjacent to the Atlantic Ocean. I even rented a boat. If I weigh you down enough, no one will ever find your body," he expounded, as he looked straight at her.

She saw the cold, dead eyes of a man who had lost his way. She saw her death when he looked at her. He really was going to kill her. *Would Michael even know where to look?*

She remembered seeing Michael before they pulled away. He said he was coming for her and for her to stay safe. She would stay safe until he found her. She would use her brains and come up with a plan until Michael could get to her. He promised to protect her, but a part of her couldn't help but doubt him now. He was left without a car. How would he ever find her in time? Ingrams had said three days. Why did he plan on keeping her alive for that specific amount of time?

Michael was five miles away from Kennebunk and in the middle of nowhere. There wasn't a car in sight. He decided to run to the town and made it in under an hour. Good thing his training and work had required him to remain extremely physically fit. He still ran every morning out of habit. Coming upon the first restaurant he found, he inquired about the nearest hotel.

"Three blocks due south," the waitress told him.

He approached the desk clerk of the Kennebunk Inn and asked for a first floor room near the emergency exit. Once inside, he sat down on the bed and placed his first call. "Rob. What the fuck is going on?" he demanded, getting up to pace in front of the window.

"What are you talking about, Michael?" Rob asked.

"You can cut the shit, Rob. I know about the GIA's involvement. I know that you had me working for a fucking terrorist organization," Michael bellowed. "How could you?"

"Look man, you don't understand," Rob pleaded.

"Make me understand. Make me understand how my best fucking friend could set me up," Michael sneered.

"They have her, man. They have Lizzie. They have the fucking love of my life," Rob groaned.

Stunned into silence, Michael sat back down on the bed.

Rob continued, "They told me if I ever wanted to see her alive again, I would find a way to deliver Emma Welby to them."

"Why didn't you just tell me that? You know I would have helped you save her."

"I know you would have, man, but I didn't have the time. I could hear her . . . I could hear her screaming in the background. I would have agreed to anything at that point. Please tell me you are still making the drop. Please tell me nothing has changed. You already received half the money," he rambled.

"I can't," Michael murmured into the phone as he hung his head. "Somebody else is in play. Some government official ran us off the road and kidnapped Emma at gunpoint. I don't know what is going on. All I know is I can't lose her. She's my angel, man," Michael confessed.

"Where are you?" Rob asked.

"The Kennebunk Inn, in Kennebunkport, about an hour south of Lewiston off of I-95," Michael continued. "Why? What do you have in mind?"

"I think it's time to do what we were trained to do. Get Lizzie and your angel back, man," Rob implored.

"Now that's the best idea you've had in a long time," Michael concurred.

"I'll call the guys and get them to haul ass to Lewiston. How fast can you make it back to my place?" Rob asked.

"Once I acquire a car, an hour tops," Michael exhaled. "And, Rob, I know some things went down between you and Tony, but we need him, man. Call him in, too."

Their Unit's Communications Sergeant, Tony, spent life before the Army as a hacker. They were going to need his particular brand of expertise if they were going to figure out where the CIA was holding Emma. She was, after all, the necessary ingredient to getting Lizzie back.

Michael walked out of the emergency exit and found the first car he tried unlocked. *People really shouldn't be so trusting.* He opened the front door and lowered himself to the floor. Thirty seconds later, the car started. He got up, hopped in, and closed the door.

Hang on, Emma. I'm coming.

CHAPTER
EIGHT

Michael parked on the street in front of a two-story colonial style house. He walked down the curved walkway to Rob's front door, rang the doorbell, and waited. Steve must have been close by, because he was already there. Michael walked in, and Rob walked straight up to him, locking his sad eyes with Michael's, silently pleading for his forgiveness.

Rob's face was flushed, and he was blinking back tears at the thought of betraying his best friend, his brother. Michael wouldn't have understood what Rob did before meeting Emma, but now he understood completely. Michael shook Rob's hand and then bumped fists. Rob pulled him into a one-arm embrace, and the men patted each other on the back.

Seeing Steve hanging back, Michael walked over to him and extended his hand, but to his surprise, Steve pulled him into a hug. It had been six months since they'd left the Army, six months since he had last seen his brothers. Still he knew, without a doubt, they would all come.

About an hour later, Tony rolled in straight from the airport. It was a good thing Rob liked his guns. His house was filled with weaponry in every corner and cabinet. All of it would come in handy for this mission.

They were missing Kevin, but they couldn't call him in on this. They all worked private security, except Kevin. Kevin was with Homeland Security. For what they had in mind, they needed to stay off the radar.

Michael and Rob briefed the men on how a terrorist cell had kidnapped Lizzie and forced Rob to find a way to deliver Emma and her knowledge of the biochemical weapon delivery system. They revealed Michael and Emma's plan to kidnap the terrorist waiting on Emma at the drop point. "Tony? How are you with a Dell laptop?" Michael asked.

"All I need is an internet connection. The equipment doesn't really matter," Tony explained.

Michael pulled Rob's laptop out of his case and handed it to Tony. "All I have is a license plate number. I need you to get me every possible piece of information you can from that. Can you do it?" Michael begged.

"Can I do it? Can I do it?" Tony bantered. "Give me the number," he demanded, all joking aside as he sat down and went online.

In under three minutes, they had a name: CIA Special Agent Daniel Ingrams.

"Why would the CIA kidnap Emma? If they wanted the prototype she was working on, all they had to do was go through the proper channels to get it," Michael wondered as he paced back and forth in front of Rob's bay window.

"What do you want me to find next? Bank statements? Property listings?" Tony asked.

"Yes," Michael replied.

Over the course of the next hour they had Ingram's bank statements, his real estate holdings, and even his career achievements with the CIA.

"I hate to ask this of you, Tony, but I don't see how it can be avoided," Michael grumbled.

"Just spit it out. You know I will do it," Tony demanded.

"I know, that's why I hate to even ask," Michael warned. "I need you to hack into the CIA database and find out what Ingrams was working on. What he would possibly want with Emma."

"The CIA, that's going to be tough. For anyone that isn't me," Tony quipped.

Michael smiled. He knew he could count on his brothers. This breach took longer than the last several. It was two more hours until Tony had information for Michael and the Unit.

"It doesn't look good, brother," Tony said as he stood so Michael could sit down and view what Tony had been looking at. Michael inhaled deeply as he realized the amount of shit they were in.

Michael explained That Special Agent Daniel Ingrams had lost a friend in Algeria to the GIA. He had worked the terrorist case for the last three years until about eight months ago when the CIA closed the case and handed the file to a junior agent to monitor chatter.

"So he is using Emma to get to the GIA?" Steve interjected.

"I don't think so," Michael responded. "Before he took her, he said he was going to kill her," Michael said as dread crept up his throat.

"If Ingrams kills Emma, the GIA will kill Lizzie. We have to stop him," Rob exclaimed, visibly shaking as he raked his hand through his hair. Lizzie was his life. She was all he talked about while on missions; getting home to his Lizzie.

"Damn right we have to stop him," Michael muttered, more to himself than to his brothers. He couldn't tell his brothers he had fallen in love with a woman over the course of two days. They would call him crazy. Still he knew he loved her. He knew it the moment Ingrams pointed a gun to her head. She created a paradox for him. Not only did she calm him, but the erotic images she set off in his imagination were driving him nuts. She affected him the way no one else could.

"So how do we find him?" asked Tony.

"We follow the money. He has to have her stashed someplace. My guess is he is not a stupid man. He's desperate, but not stupid. So he wouldn't take her to some place he owns," Steve answered calmly from the kitchen table, tapping his fingers against its glass top.

"Let's go through his bank and credit card statements. Maybe we'll get lucky," Steve interjected.

God, Michael hoped so. They had gotten lucky in the past. Still it wouldn't hurt to say a little prayer. So, for the first time since he left Afghanistan, he prayed.

"I found something," Steve exclaimed.

"What is it?" Rob asked.

"Ingrams rented a cabin on his Visa card. He rented it for six nights, and those six nights began yesterday," Steve explained, waving the piece of printer paper in his hand.

Clearly, Ingrams didn't expect anyone to be following him. He certainly didn't expect Michael and his brothers to be tracking him down.

They had been at it for a good two hours, printing all of his statements for the last eight months. They had been searching for anything that might lead them in his direction. Now they had it.

"Where is it?" Michael asked.

"Wells, Maine. We're going to Wells. "We got damn lucky. That's only an hour drive at the most," Steve said.

"Grab the gear," Michael commanded. While Tony had been searching the internet, the rest of the men had been packing as much weaponry and ammunition as they could carry. Each man picked up a bag and made his way out the front door, down the front walk to the street. They were going to have to take two cars and find a cargo van later. Each man threw a gear bag in the trunk of the two cars.

"Guys, follow me down the street. I have to ditch this car," Michael requested.

They hopped in the cars, started the engines, and followed Michael into town. Michael pulled into an abandoned alleyway and wiped his fingerprints from the car. He jumped into the passenger side of Rob's car. The caravan of men started rolling down highway I-95 to Wells . . . to Emma.

CLOSER

I'm coming, Emma. Hold on, Michael thought.

CHAPTER NINE

A damp, musty smell assaulted her senses. A single, bare light bulb hung in front of her, glaring into her eyes. Emma tried to peer around the room. Against the far wall, an old green couch sat on the concrete floor. The stairs were behind her. She was in a cellar of a house, her hands tied to one of the exposed, old wooden beams that ran the length of the ceiling. When she looked up, she could see the wiring and cables. *Did he live here?*

"Don't you touch me, you freak," Emma screamed.

"You are going to tell me everything I want to know about your boyfriend before I kill you," Ingrams commanded as he ran his finger between her breasts.

Emma wiggled and tossed her body away from Ingram's hand.

"Who is he, Ms. Welby?" Ingrams demanded.

"Go to hell!" Emma exclaimed as she spat in his direction.

He didn't take kindly to the insult. Ingrams raised his right hand and backhanded her hard across her face. Her lip busted open, and she sucked in the familiar metallic taste of blood.

"We can play this game all night. In fact, we can play this game for the next three nights. But I guarantee you, you will tell me what I want to know. The question is, Ms. Welby, how quickly do you want to die?" Ingrams jeered as he wiped the line of blood trickling from Emma's lip down her chin. Ingrams moved his face closer to Emma's and licked at the blood.

"You've obviously suffered some kind of psychotic break, you sick man. You said you worked for the CIA. I don't know anybody that works for the CIA that would treat a fellow colleague the way you're treating me," Emma snarled as she swung her legs away from Ingram's body.

"Tell me about him. How long have you known him? Does he know about the work you do for the DOD? Does he know about Project Hummingbird?" Ingrams growled as he punched Emma in the stomach.

She couldn't lean forward to block the pain. Her hands were bound above her head and her body was dangling, her feet swinging above the floor.

"Come on, sweetie. Make my work easy for me. Don't put yourself through this unnecessary pain. Just tell me who he is and who he works for, and we can be done here," he said as he pulled his arm back to ram his fist into her stomach a second time.

Emma felt the wind leave her body. Her eyes glistened with unshed tears. He would not break her. If she told him what he wanted to know, she was dead. She had to endure whatever he dished out, just until Michael could save her.

98

He raised his arm again to strike her, but this time, she lifted her leg and connected with his groin.

"You bitch," he huffed as he hunched over in pain.

There, that would buy her a reprieve, she thought, just enough to gain some of her strength back. She needed to be strong for Michael. Shit, she needed to be strong for herself.

After rolling on the floor in utter agony for several minutes, Ingrams got to his knees and pushed himself upright. "I am going to kill him with or without your help, Ms. Welby," Ingrams seethed.

He went to the bag he brought with him and pulled out the duct tape. He walked behind her and wrestled her legs together as she kicked and bucked. He finally managed to hold them tightly and began rolling the tape around her ankles, binding both legs.

"There, no more kicking." He smiled as he stood up and placed the tape back in his bag.

He turned and walked back over to her. Her hands felt like they were separating from her wrists, but she couldn't give up. How long would he take to kill her? Did he really plan on torturing her first? It was obvious something wasn't right with this man.

"I must say, Ms. Welby, I didn't expect you to be so strong. You have a PhD for God's sake. But you're also delicate like a flower," Ingrams told her as he ran his hand between her legs. He wriggled his hand in between her thighs and cupped her sex. She squirmed and bucked, but she couldn't escape him.

"Get your hands off of me!" she yelled as tears fell down her cheeks. Salt mixed with the metal taste on her lips.

"Maybe I will have you before I kill you. You are a remarkably beautiful woman, Ms. Welby," he insisted as he applied pressure to her clit with his nubby fingers.

"You'd like that, you sick animal? Why don't you untie me so we can become properly acquainted," she retorted as she tried to again free herself from his hand. *Where are you Michael?*

"Oh, Emma, Emma. Whatever shall I do with you?" he asked as he removed his hand from her sex. "I can't let you help a terrorist organization. I have to kill you. What you know is too valuable. They won't stop coming after you until you give them what they want. And they want information on Project Hummingbird. You really can't expect me, a CIA agent, to let you go now, can you?" Ingrams coaxed while he brushed Emma's reddened face with the back of his hand.

He lowered his arm, pulled back his fist, and punched her square in the face. "That's for kicking me in the balls, you bitch."

Tears welled in her eyes and leaked down her face. Blood was running from her nose, dripping onto the concrete floor. He turned his back to her.

"I have to go put the boat in the water and bring it to the dock at the back of the cottage. I won't be gone long. Then we will continue with our little chat," he said with a singsong voice as he walked away towards the stairs. "Stay here and be a good girl." He smiled, walking up the stairs to the front room of the cottage.

Emma's head dropped, shot through with pain, and she sobbed at her hopeless situation. The man planned on *killing* her. She could only hope Michael was on his way. But the truth was, she knew he wouldn't be able to find her. Ingrams didn't bother to cover her eyes when they arrived. She saw the cottage surrounded by trees and ocean. They were back in the woods, away from people. There was no one around to hear her scream.

She began wondering how he would kill her. Would he rape her first? He certainly touched her like he was going to violate her. She knew he wanted information. *That* she could work to her advantage. She knew she was strong. She could withstand it . . . until she couldn't. Would she turn on Michael then? Would she tell Ingrams everything he wanted to know and get Michael killed in the process? No, she couldn't think like that. She had to hold out as long as she could to give Michael a chance to find her. She had to believe he would find her, or she might as well accept her death. Only she wasn't ready to die. She wanted a life. She wanted to finish her project. She wanted to see where her feelings for Michael would take her.

The caravan of men continued down highway I-95 and approached the Wells city exit. Rob exited and drove down a two-lane country road, passing high-priced mansions.

"Should we drive by? See who's home?" Rob asked Michael as he made a left onto Dock Street.

"Yeah. Let's do a little reconnaissance work before we go in guns blazing," Michael responded as he tried to concentrate on the mission before him. He couldn't let himself think Emma had already been killed. She had been taken from him over five hours ago. It was now nearing 1630 hours, and the sun hadn't yet started to set. They still had functional daylight. Emma was still alive. She was a smart, tough woman. She had to be. He cleared his mind of Emma as Rob pointed out the upcoming cottage.

"This is it," Rob said as he slowed to pass the house.

"This can't be right," Michael responded, "there are no cars here."

"Maybe he isn't here," Rob stated.

"Don't even think that way. She has to be here," Michael hissed.

"The customer service agent said this was the address of the rental under Ingrams' name," Rob remarked.

"Pull over up here, in that turnabout," Michael commanded. "We'll double back and check it out anyways."

Rob pulled over into the thicket of trees, and Steve pulled behind him. Tony and Steve got out of the second car and walked over. They stood in a circle with a serious look in their eyes. They were ready for action. They had missed it the six months since they'd left the Army. Danger was all they knew until six months ago. Keeping a state of hypervigilance in a combat zone became second nature. Hell, they were still hyper vigilant.

"There was no car at the residence, but I want to check it out anyways given the Intel we have on the place," Michael explained to his brothers.

"We might as well. We're here," Tony said as he walked back to his rental car and popped the trunk.

Michael and Rob grabbed their bags. Once they all had their gear, they set them on the ground and pulled out the weapons they would be using to search the house. Tony passed out the ear pieces to each member of the Unit.

"Locked and loaded," Steve grinned. He felt a pure adrenaline rush flood him just like in any mission he undertook. Just because he was no longer an active Green Beret didn't mean he didn't feel the same type of rush he felt in Afghanistan. They ran the chance of being killed. In fact, on all of the private security details they worked, they ran that same chance. They placed their bags back into the trunks of their vehicles and started the quarter-mile trek back to the cottage.

"Tony and Steve, you have the sniper rifles. You take up position in the surrounding woods with sights on the front and back door in case anyone tries to escape. I'll go in soft. And Rob, I want you on my six in case I need you in there," Michael finished.

They reached the cottage and disappeared into the woods. No one would know they were even there.

"Comm check," Tony said into his shirt.

One by one, each member of the Unit checked in with Tony. Communications were working. One less thing for Michael to worry about. He didn't know why he was worrying so much anyways. He trusted these men with his life. But this time, it wasn't just his own life. It was Emma's life, too. He had to clear his mind. He had to prepare himself for whatever he might find lying in that cottage, and that included Emma's lifeless body.

Rob followed Michael to the back door. Michael picked the lock in less than thirty seconds and slid his tools back into his shirt pocket. He twisted the doorknob and quietly opened the door. He stood there for one full minute, listening for any indication of the whereabouts of the occupants. Just because there wasn't a car, didn't mean there wasn't someone there. Ingrams could have ditched the very obvious SUV.

After a full minute, Michael treaded lightly inside the kitchen. He stopped again, listening for any hint of movement. Nothing. He cleared the kitchen and made his way, up against the wall, to the entrance to the living room. Again he waited and listened. Silence. He rounded the living room and went into the hall, pausing. When he was certain there was no one in the rest of the first floor, he opened the bedroom door.

"All clear," he radioed to the men.

He walked back into the kitchen and stood next to the door, which led to the basement. He knew that opening it could give away his position. So he stood silently listening and praying for some sign of Emma. He placed his ear against the door and waited. He heard her then, softly sobbing. Overcome with emotion, Michael opened the door and took the stairs two at a time. He could be walking into a trap, but he didn't care. He had to get to her. At the bottom of the stairs, his heart sank into his stomach.

There she was hanging from the rafters, alive. He went to her and cupped her face with his hands. "Emma, baby. Look at me. I'm here. You're all right now," he coaxed her as he took stock of her injuries. "Tell me where you're hurt, Emma," he whispered. Seeing her beaten and bloody was more than his heart could take. His eyes glistened as he looked over her body, her busted nose and lip. Her beautiful face marred with such injury.

"My stomach hurts, Michael," Emma whimpered, "my nose hurts, too."

"Don't worry, Emma, I've got you. No one is going to hurt you again," Michael said to her as he reached up to untie her hands.

"Rob, get down here, man. I need you. Emma's hurt," he said into his shirt.

He heard his best friend taking the same stairs two at a time.

"Let's get her down," Rob asserted as he finished untying her hands and releasing them from above her head.

She collapsed into Michael. Michael's arm wrapped around her waist and held her up. He scooped her up in his arms and carried her to the couch, gently laying her down. He stood back to give Rob room to work. Rob lifted Emma's shirt and pointed out the bruises which were already starting to form.

"Fuck. I'll kill 'em. I'll fucking kill 'em," Michael snapped, running his hand roughly over his stubble.

Her porcelain skin was marred by bruises some fuckwad inflicted on her. Michael felt a rage he had never known. He was going to kill Ingrams. Michael knelt down next to the couch.

"He wanted me to tell him about you, but I didn't," she said proudly to Michael as he grasped her hand in his. He took care with it as it was discolored from having been tied at such an angle for such a long time. He rubbed her hand, trying to increase the circulation.

"What do you mean, Emma? What did he want? What did he say to you?" Michael asked as he continued to rub her hand lightly.

"He wanted to know who you were and who you worked for. He said he is going to kill you, Michael," Emma sobbed as she squeezed Michael's hand. "He said he is going to kill me so that I can't give information to the GIA," she whimpered.

"He's not going to hurt you ever again, Emma. I will take care of you," he promised as he bent his head and kissed her ever so gently on her lips, tasting her blood. He had made her a promise he had never made to another living being.

"Where is he, Emma?" Rob asked, pulling her shirt back down.

"He said he had to pull the boat up to the dock," she sobbed, "so he can throw me into the ocean."

"Let's get her out of here, man, before he comes back," Rob said. "We can deal with him later, but we have to get her taken care of first. Make sure there are no serious injuries. Let's get her back to my house where I can bandage her up."

Rob understood how his friend felt. His Lizzie was still out there. God only knew what was happening to her. The quicker they could get Emma bandaged up, the quicker they could get Lizzie back.

Michael picked her up in his arms and carried her up the stairs. Emma wrapped her arms around Michael's neck, buried her face in his chest, and silently cried. He had come for her against all odds. She didn't even know how he found her, but he promised and he did.

He carried her to Rob's car and placed her carefully into the backseat. Michael got in the back with her and put her head on his lap as Rob drove them back to his house. Tony and Steve followed in the car behind. Yes, they would take care of Special Agent Daniel Ingram, but not tonight. Tonight, they would take care of Emma.

CLOSER

CHAPTER TEN

They pulled up to Rob's house and parked on the street. Michael had been stroking Emma's hair as she lay in his lap.

"We're here, baby. Don't move. Let me carry you in," he softened and opened the car door.

"I can walk, Michael, really," she responded and sat up slowly, placing her feet on the floorboard of the car.

Michael ran around to her side of the car and opened the door for her. He reached in to carry her, but she started to stand of her own free will. He placed his hand at her elbow to gently move her away from the car as he slammed the door. Stepping beside her, he placed his hand on the small of her back and led her down the walkway to the front door. Once inside, Michael guided her to the couch.

"Why don't you lie down? You have been through enough," he whispered behind her as he helped guide her to a sitting position.

"Really, Michael, I'm just sore," she pleaded. "That's all. I promise, if I was really hurt, I would tell you."

Rob made his way to the couch and effectively crowded Michael off to the side. Michael sat at the end of the couch so he could watch what Rob was doing. He didn't want her hurt, and he knew his friend wouldn't hurt her if it could be avoided. Rob brought out the antiseptic and a cotton ball.

"Hold still. This is going to burn," he cautioned, bringing his hand up to the cut on her lip.

He dabbed her cut lightly, and she winced. He began blowing on the cut to ease the burn.

"Should you be doing that, man? What about germs?" Michael asked as he bounced his knee impatiently up and down.

"Since when did you stop trusting me, Michael?" Rob asked, although his latest stunt—getting Michael to unknowingly work for a terrorist cell—could make anyone lose faith.

"I trust you. I just don't want her hurt worse than she is."

Next, Rob moved to her nose. He pressed both sides of it with his thumbs, gauging her reaction. She winced and fought back her tears. He had to give this girl credit. She was tough.

"It's not broken, but it will be sore for a few days," he told Emma as he dabbed the cotton to remove the dried blood from her nostrils.

"What about your stomach? How are you feeling here," he asked her as he placed a hand against her belly.

Michael couldn't stand to see someone touch his woman. For all intents and purposes, she was his, and the only person who should be touching her was him. But his mind knew Rob had to examine her.

"Here, sit back and let me see," Rob commanded and gently pushed her shoulders back against the couch. He lifted her shirt and could see the blossoming of a bruise over her right rib cage. He pressed with his fingers, and she groaned in pain.

"Stop it, man. You're hurting her," Michael demanded as he sprung to his feet, pushing Rob away from Emma. Rob fell over but caught himself with his hand.

"Boy, do you have it bad," Rob said to himself as he stood up.

"What can I do for you, Emma?" Michael whispered, lowering himself next to her on the couch.

"I would really love a shower. I need to wash him away," she said, looking at Michael with relief in her eyes. He had come for her. She still couldn't believe it. "How did you find me?" she asked Michael, never breaking eye contact.

"It's a long story. How about I help you get a hot shower, and then we get these guys to fix us something to eat. You have to be starving, and Tony is one hell of a cook. What do you say?" His eyes pleaded with hers.

"That sounds like heaven," she cooed, struggling to stand.

Michael held her elbow as he helped her up.

"Just point me in the direction of the shower," she said.

"I'll show you," he replied, guiding her by the elbow into the kitchen where his brothers had gathered.

"Tony, what would it take to get you to cook us up something to eat?" Michael smiled from across the room.

"I'd be happy to, as long as Rob here has something in this place for me to work with," Tony said, looking at Rob for a response.

"Sure do. What are you guys in the mood for? I have hamburger patties or Tilapia," Rob answered, looking at Emma.

"I am so hungry, I could eat anything. I am not picky. Whatever is easier for you, Tony."

Her broken smile caught Tony's eye. Tony could see that sparkle in Emma's eye returning. She wasn't gravely injured. He had seen gravely injured. A hot shower and a good meal and she would be fine. It was no wonder Michael was so protective of Emma. She was a beautiful woman. If Michael hadn't claimed her, Tony would have taken his shot. He loved the way her blue eyes conveyed her feelings. He could tell Emma was smitten with Michael when she turned her head to look at him for his opinion on dinner.

"Why don't you cook the fish? It's too cold outside to cook on the grill. Rob, if you don't mind, Emma would like to take a shower," Michael baited, waiting for Rob's approval.

"Sure, man. You know where it is. Clean towels and washrags are in the cupboard. Let me grab you Lizzie's shampoo and conditioner for Emma," he said as he walked upstairs to the master bathroom.

He met Emma and Michael in the hallway outside of the bathroom. He handed the shampoo and conditioner to Emma and said, "Dinner will be ready in forty-five minutes. Take your time." He turned and went back downstairs, leaving Michael and Emma alone together for the first time since early that morning.

"I want to help you, if you'll let me," Michael said, his breath close to Emma's ear.

Emma felt shivers run down her spine. Something about the proximity to Michael touched her. It was as if he reached through her body and took hold of her heart.

"I really am okay, Michael. You can stop worrying," she said, stepping into the bathroom with her hand on the door. She went to close the door, but Michael stopped her by putting his hand against it.

"I don't think you understand, Emma. I need to touch you, to know you are really here. You scared the shit out of me when you got into the car with Ingrams. I didn't know what to do. I thought I was going crazy. Please, Emma, let me take care of you," he confessed through the two inch crack in the door.

She exhaled as if she had been holding her breath and opened the door, silently inviting him in. He couldn't help but wonder if she wanted him in there with her or if she was just appeasing him because he had saved her life. He didn't care. Either way he was going to get to touch her again, and touching her again was what he wanted to do since that morning.

Emma stood nervously next to the sink. Michael stalked closer to her. When he was in her personal space, he reached down and grabbed the hem of her shirt.

"Can you lift your arms for me, Emma?" he whispered.

Emma raised her arms above her head, and Michael slowly peeled her sweater from her body. She lowered her arms and stood trembling in front of him. He gently reached around her back, taking care to brush his fingers against her skin as he went, and unclasped her blue lace bra, pulling it down her arms and placing it on the sink. She shivered like a small and frightened animal.

Michael ran his fingers down between her breasts to the top of her jeans. He used both hands to unbutton her pants. Her breath caught in her throat. She met his hooded, wanton gaze as he slid the zipper down. He ran his hands under the material of her jeans and pushed them to the floor. His rough hands felt so good going down her soft legs. When he reached the bottom, he kneeled in front of her, his head at her stomach. He leaned in and gently kissed the bruises as if he could lift the pain away.

He bent slightly forward and picked up her right foot. He pulled her jeans over her foot and set it back on the floor. He repeated the process with her left foot. She stood in nothing but her blue lacey panties. He deliberately caressed her sides with his hands.

"Did I hurt you, Emma?" he breathed against her skin, running his lips over her stomach as it quivered from his touch.

"No," she moaned.

She felt the fire heat her core and a throbbing pulse between her legs.

He hooked his thumbs in the sides of her panties and slowly pulled them down to her feet. He pressed another kiss to her stomach before standing. He gazed at her, backing away to admire the view. He loved her body exactly the way she was. Her breasts, large and shapely. Her soft stomach would be the perfect place to rest his head after a long day. And her hips. He couldn't wait to get a hold of her hips and drive her into oblivion. Her body was his temple.

Emma looked up at him through lowered lashes. He removed his shirt, revealing his washboard stomach and broad chest. He had the perfect amount of hair on his chest and the happy trail he had led down into his pants. He bent forward to remove his boots and then his socks. He was really going to get in the shower with her. She didn't know what to do or what to say, so she kept her mouth closed and watched as he unbuttoned his pants and pushed them to a pile around his feet. He stepped out, and she could see his erection through his boxer briefs. When he removed them, she lost her breath. His erection was so hard, his cock was reaching up towards his navel. She could see a wet bead of liquid on the head of his cock. How she longed to taste him, lick that bead right from his velvety head. His veins were bulging, and she wondered how sore he must be from being so hard.

He pushed back the shower curtain and turned the faucet on hot. When the water was to temperature, he motioned for her to enter. Her hands reached up to cover herself from his penetrating eyes. He pulled her arms away and placed them against her side. "You are so beautiful. Please don't ever hide from me," he begged her as he placed his hand on the small of her back to guide her into the shower.

She twisted her fingers together in front of her and bit down on her lower lip softly. Michael wanted nothing more than to bite that bottom lip for her. He gently brushed his thumb over her injured bottom lip and pulled it from her teeth. A growl escaped from deep within his throat. She hadn't been with a man in a really long time. Was she ready to be with him?

She stepped into the shower and he followed. He let her stand under the water while he watched the steam rise from her body and water flow down over her taut nipples. He picked up the washcloth and lathered it with soap, bringing it to her stomach. He made quick, gentle work of washing her stomach but spent a great deal more time soaping up her breasts. He palmed one breast in his hand as it glided over her soapy soft skin. He rolled the taut nipple between his thumb and finger, and she moaned his name. He went harder still.

"Turn around," he said, and she did as he bid.

He lowered himself to his knees and washed her back, spending a glorious amount of time washing her ass, thighs, and hips. He stood as she rinsed the soap from her body. He grabbed the shampoo bottle and poured some into his hands. He lathered his hands and then began washing her hair.

No one had ever touched her like this before. She was falling apart in his hands, melting at his touch. He rinsed her hair and then conditioned it. Once he was done, he pulled her wet body to his. She pressed her chest to touch his, flesh against flesh. God, did she want him. She didn't want to wait any longer. His mouth met hers and he adored her. He poured every feeling he had for her into that slow, soft kiss. She was melting into a pool at his feet.

Her legs grew weak, but this time, instead of grabbing her waist to hold her up, Michael grabbed her thighs and squeezed. He continued to palm her thighs as he probed her mouth with his tongue. His hard cock was pressed against her stomach. She moved down just a little bit and allowed his hard cock to run between her large breasts, the conditioner creating a perfect lubricant. She moved up and down, creating a sheath for his cock between her breasts. He froze.

"Fuck, Emma," he growled from deep within his throat. "Not yet, baby," he admonished.

He pulled away from her and murmured something under his breath as he got out of the shower. What had she done wrong? He grabbed a towel and motioned for her to get out of the shower, too. She did, and he took care to dry off every droplet of water. She couldn't understand what he was waiting for. Why didn't he take her in the shower? She had made it painfully clear she wanted him. Why was he waiting?

"What's wrong?" she coaxed, uncertain, as he continued to dry her off with the towel.

"Everything's right. For once, everything's fucking right, and I don't want to fuck it up," he said. "Don't get me wrong, I want you. In the worst. Fucking. Way." He leaned in and kissed her lightly, taking care not to hurt her busted lip. "But I am not going to take you after what you have been through today. You need to rest, and I won't hurt you." He slid his pants back on.

She stood dumbfounded as she realized not only were they physically attracted to each other, but he also stimulated her mind, and he respected her knowledge. He knew the depth of who she was, and she was in deep.

They made their way back downstairs to the dinner table with wet heads. All of the guys smiled at Michael with knowing eyes. Michael gave them the look that said, "Don't say a word." Rob had set the table, and Tony was just finishing with the Tilapia. Everything smelled so good. She couldn't remember the last time she ate. Michael pulled a chair out for her and he sat in the chair next to her touching her leg with his . . . *He had to be touching her.*

"Someone has to say it," Rob said as he passed the fish to the left. "We need a plan to get Lizzie back."

"Who's Lizzie?" Emma asked.

"Lizzie is my fiancée, and the GIA have her," Rob confided.

"Oh my God, Rob. That's awful. What can I do?" Emma asked.

"We need a plan," Rob said, his voice choking over the thought of his fiancée held prisoner by the terrorists.

"We can still make the drop as planned," Emma said as everyone paused mid-bite to stare in disbelief. "Think about it. It's me they want, and I feel safe that you won't let anything happen to me," she said to all of the men at the table.

It was Michael that responded, "Damn right we won't. No one will ever take you from me again," he said in front of his brothers, clearing up any remaining doubt at the table as to whom Emma belonged.

They talked over dinner, devising their plan to capture Ahmed El-Amin, keep Emma safe, and rescue Lizzie.

They still had a two-day drive in front of them. They would drive eight hours tomorrow, stop at a hotel for the night, and drive the remaining three hours in the morning. That way, they would be well-rested for this most important mission. Everything had to go according to plan or they risked losing Lizzie. All it would take is Ahmed making one phone call, and Rob would never see her again. Michael had never gotten what Rob and Lizzie had, not until he met his Emma. Now he understood: Lizzie was Rob's air, his life force, the same way Emma was his.

CLOSER

Early the next morning, the caravan of former
Green Berets, plus Emma, drove until they reached
Harrisburg. There, they pulled into the parking lot of
the Hampton Inn. It had been a long nine-hour drive
from Lewiston, having only stopped for gas, for
something to eat, and for the occasional bathroom
break. Michael made sure he and Emma got their own
room. He carried their bags upstairs and placed them
on the bench inside the door. Emma followed him into
the room. The first thing to catch her attention was one
king size bed.

"A little presumptuous, don't cha think?" she
playfully asked Michael as she pulled him in for a hug.
This was the first time she had asserted herself with
Michael and it felt good to touch him anytime she
wanted. Now, maybe she was being too presumptuous.
She pulled quickly back from him like his body burned
her and made her way to the window, wrapping her
arms around herself. She looked out on the darkening
parking lot, lost in her head again. Maybe she
shouldn't have been so forward as to hug him. Maybe
he didn't like being touched like that. He walked up

behind her and nuzzled her neck as he wrapped his strong arms around her waist.

"What's wrong? Why did you stop?" he asked as he inhaled her unique scent.

"I was just thinking," she responded despondently.

"Don't worry about tomorrow. I promise nothing will happen to you. My brothers and I will keep you safe," he said reassuringly, hoping to calm her fears.

"It's not that," she whispered facing the window. "I trust you and the guys to keep me safe."

"Then what is it?" he asked, confused.

"I was just thinking maybe I shouldn't be so forward with you. That isn't like me, you know, to come on to a guy. I don't know what came over me to hug you that way," she confessed.

"What? Emma, you can hug me anytime you want. In fact, I would prefer you touch me anytime you want and as often as you can," he whispered into her ear, causing goose bumps to rise on her flesh and a tingle to spread down her spine.

He nipped at her earlobe, playfully trying to pull her out of her head and back into her body. She turned in his arms and pressed herself against his hard, broad chest.

"I'm just afraid I am going to get lost in you," she said, hope filling her eyes.

"I'm already lost in you," he confided, lowering his mouth to her neck.

He bit at her neck and then kissed the spot to soothe his bite.

"Maybe this is moving too fast, Michael," she said, tilting her head to allow him better access to her throat.

If she didn't get out of her head, she was going to ruin the mood. Michael didn't allow that to happen. He was sucking on her neck, and she was moaning his name as her flesh caught fire from his touch. His palm made its way under her shirt. He squeezed her breast, and her nipples tightened. He rolled her nipple through the silk of her bra between his thumb and forefinger. His other hand moved over her back, down to her derriere. He cupped and squeezed her ass, pulling her closer to him so she could feel his erection pressing against her belly.

"Michael," she whispered into the air. "I've never needed anyone this way, and I'm scared."

That was all Michael needed to hear. He picked her up and said, "Wrap your legs around my waist." She did and was carried to the bed. He laid her tenderly upon the mattress. He reached down, unbuttoned her jeans, and pulled them off her body. "Sit up and raise your arms," he ordered, removing her shirt.

She did and then she reached behind her back, slowly removing her bra, teasing him.

Michael groaned and pushed her shoulders back until she was lying on the bed again. He stood to take in his beautiful Emma. He gazed deeply into her bright, electric blue eyes, hoping to convey the depth of the feelings he concealed. He reached for the bottom of his Henley and pulled it over his head.

Emma stared, blushing at the thought of what might happen. He removed his pants and underwear with one move, stepping out of the pool of clothing at the bottom of his feet. He grabbed a condom from his wallet. Stalking her like a predator, he kneeled onto the bed. He began stroking her calf with his rough fingers, his eyes perusing his way up her leg. He traced the outline of her panties, sliding his finger just inside the lace. She moaned and arched under his touch as he brushed closer to her nub. She gasped when he suddenly tore the panties from her body and brought them to his nose, inhaling her scent.

When he got his fill, he tossed her panties into the pile of clothes at the foot of the bed and pushed her legs apart, never breaking eye contact. He watched her through hooded eyes as he lowered himself to her core. Parting her folds with his fingers, he startled her when he licked his way slowly from the bottom of her clit to the top. He slid a finger inside her dripping wet core. His erection grew even bigger at the feel of her arousal. He continued circling and licking her clit, applying pressure while he slid another finger inside her tight walls. He moved his fingers out slowly and then pushed them back into her again while he suckled on her clit.

Arching her back off of the bed, she pushed herself closer to his mouth. *Didn't she dream of this happening?* She wrapped her hands in his soft, curly hair, pulling his mouth closer. She moved his head with her hands, directing his tongue where to go. She felt powerful, a heady mix of sensations she had never experienced before. This man was worshipping her. At that thought, she felt herself climbing higher and higher until she was at her peak. But before she could climax, he stopped. She moaned with the withdrawal of his fingers.

"We come together, baby," he spoke in a husky voice.

He grabbed the condom and ripped open the foil package, unrolling it over his hard cock. He climbed atop her and braced himself with his forearms against the mattress to keep from crushing her so that he could look directly into her bright blue eyes. He was taken aback by the desire and passion he saw reflected back at him. He had to make it clear to her that she wasn't just another woman to him. He had to make it clear…she was it for him.

"When I enter you, you're mine," he challenged. "That's it. There's no turning back. Do you understand? You're mine."

"I'm already yours, Michael. Please," she begged him.

She wanted to feel his body flush against hers. She wanted to give his hard muscles a soft place to rest. She pulled him down onto her so there was nothing separating them, not even air. She couldn't get close enough to him. She reached up and grabbed his ass, trying to pull him closer. He just stared at her. He moved and placed his cock at her entrance. He started to push himself inside of her, and she gasped at how large he was. He stretched her walls to the limit.

Michael moaned at how tight she was as he covered himself with her. He paused, allowing her body to acclimate to his size.

She was having none of it. She titled and angled her hips to allow him to fully penetrate her. He was as deep as he could go, fully sheathed. She could feel his balls against her ass. He pulled out and slowly drove into her again and again. Her hands caressed the muscles on his back. She ran her fingernails down his muscles tracing each hard sinew. Cupping his ass, she licked and sucked at his neck. He brought his mouth to hers and kissed her.

"Michael please," she begged. "I need you harder."

He pulled himself all but out of her and then slammed into her with a force she felt at the very root of her being. He continued his onslaught into her, slamming and thrusting, driving her higher and higher. She tilted and rocked her hips, rubbing her clit against his pelvis in time with his thrusts.

"Please don't stop," she begged.

He was breathing hard against her neck as he slammed into her again and again. The man was pushing her higher than she had ever known. With the last thrust, she reached the pinnacle of pleasure, her body bursting into white stars behind her closed eyes as she melted into the mattress. She screamed his name.

He felt her tighten and convulse around his cock and knew she had found her release. He was holding on for his life to make sure he pleasured her so that with one more push, he found his own release in her. His body tensed, and he moaned her name before dropping his full weight onto her. She continued to caress his back as he came back down from the highest point of his life. Once would not be enough with Emma. Forever would not be enough with Emma. *What was he going to do?* He quickly got up and disposed of the condom. He returned to the bed and scooted her up so her head was resting against his sweaty chest.

"That was amazing, Emma," he said as he ran his fingers lazily up and down her arm. That was the last thing he remembered.

He awoke rested and in awe of the woman in his arms. He gently kissed her forehead, and she opened her sleepy eyes. Their eyes met and she smiled up at him and kissed his lips. He wrapped his hand in her hair and brought her mouth closer to his. He deepened the kiss.

Before long, she pulled back and said, "I need to take a shower."

"I'll join you. I need one, too," he bantered, smiling down at her.

She removed her leg from his and got up, feeling vulnerable. Starting to cover herself up again, she remembered how he called her beautiful and looked at him. It was as though he could read her mind.

"You are honestly beautiful, Emma. I could look at you all day long." He smiled as she walked to her duffle bag to get her toiletries. "And that ass. The things I want to do with that fine, luscious ass of yours," he growled.

Maybe she should be afraid, but she wasn't. The truth was, she wanted anything he had to give her.

He laid in bed and thought about how lucky he was to have found such an amazingly smart, beautiful, courageous woman. She was willing to use herself as bait to catch a terrorist. What other woman had ever trusted in Michael so completely that she would be willing to put her life in his hands? He would value her gift to him as long as he lived. He was going to enjoy Emma with every breath he took. He didn't know how he was going to convince her, but she was it for him.

Michael felt what it was like to be inside her warm, wet body and knew he had to do it again. He waited until he heard the shower running before getting out of bed. He pushed open the bathroom door and steam billowed out into the small hallway of the hotel room. He pulled back the curtain and stepped into the shower. She was lathering up her hair so he took full advantage of her exposed breasts. He bent over and suckled her taut nipple into his mouth, gently nipping and tugging at it. His hands roamed the expanse of her body, down her arms, over her stomach, over her ass, cupping and squeezing as he went.

He moved to her other breast, paying it the same respect. He ran his hand up between her legs and cupped her sex, pressing his finger in slow circles against her clit. When she finished rinsing her hair, she splayed her fingers over his broad shoulder muscles.

She bent forward and licked the droplets of water from his chest. She bit his erect nipples and swirled her tongue around them. Michael rumbled his satisfaction. She licked her way down onto her knees, the water running in rivulets down Michael's body. She grabbed his hard, velvety cock in her hands, and he locked eyes with her. She watched him watch her as she slowly brought his cock to her lips. She teased him by licking the velvety tip with her tongue and running his head over her wet lips. She flicked the sensitive underside of his head with her tongue. He watched her as his cock disappeared into her mouth. She pulled long and hard, using her hand to follow it up. She opened her throat, taking him deep inside. He had to control himself and think of anything but what Emma was doing to him or he would come in her mouth. It felt breathtaking when she opened her throat and sucked him. Her eyes sparkled with mischief as she continued sucking.

"Fuck. Emma, baby, you have to stop. I'm going to come in your mouth, and I want you with me when I come," he told her as he tugged her up.

With one step, he pushed her up against the shower wall, hot water falling down around them. "Wrap your legs around my waist," he commanded as he lifted her into the air. He brought her down and impaled her with his cock. To his surprise, she was ready for him. He slid the entire way inside her, going as deep as possible. She wrapped her legs tighter around his waist, digging her heels into his ass, urging him to go deeper. He moved himself in and out of her at a quick pace. He thrust into her again and again. She was meeting his thrusts with her own. Her arms wound around his neck as he pushed her to the brink.

"Fuck!" she screamed.

He smiled. It did something to him to hear dirty words come out of her beautiful, pouty mouth. It took all of his willpower to keep from coming.

"Talk dirty to me," he demanded.

At his words, she went into her head again. She didn't know what to say. She had never spoken naughty words before, let alone to a man. "You make me feel good," she said as she felt her face heat.

"Say something a little dirtier to me, Emma. Tell me how I feel inside you," Michael cajoled.

This time her body was kicking in. How did he feel inside her? How could she answer that question and give him what he wanted? "Your penis feels very good inside of my vagina," she said with the same amount of trepidation and the same heating of her face.

His rhythm was increasing. He was pulling her out of her head and back into her body. "Tell me. Use dirty words, Emma. It does something to me to hear dirty words come out of that perfect, pouty mouth of yours," Michael demanded as he pumped with more force than before.

She knew what he wanted, she just had to say it. She mustered up the courage and told him how she really felt, "Your cock feels exceptional inside my pussy." The bands on her soul finally released as the naughty words left her mouth.

Hearing the nasty words come from her lips while they were having sex was more than he could take.

"Come with me," he commanded as he drove into her harder and faster.

"I'm there!" she yelled as she shattered into a million tiny pieces, pulsating around his cock. He drove into her one last time and his body went rigid with his orgasm.

"Fuck, Emma," he growled as he found his own release. He kept her pinned against the wall, afraid his own legs would give out as he came back down from his high.

He lowered her legs to the floor, keeping his hands on her waist to make sure she could stand. He brought his lips to hers and kissed her passionately. He conveyed all the emotion he was feeling for her in that one kiss. She must have felt it, too, because she was kissing him back as good as she got. He swallowed her moan, thinking about how he could never let her go. Since he met her, he slept three nights now with no nightmares. A life without her was not possible for him. She soothed his soul.

"Emma." He said her name like a prayer. "I need you to know that I will never, ever let anything happen to you again. I fucked up with Ingrams, but I swear on my life from this point forward, you do not need to worry. They will have to kill me before getting to you," he continued as he cupped her face in his hands.

She locked onto his eyes, feeling the sincerity of his words in her heart. "I believe you," she said, staring up at him.

She knew he would protect her, but what about after she was out of danger? She got the feeling he lived for danger—he was an adrenaline junkie. What about after her life went back to normal, would he still call her his?

CHAPTER TWELVE

He stood outside of the shower naked, waiting on her with a towel. She stepped outside and he took his time drying her off. "You must be starved," he said as he dried her feet.

"I could definitely eat," she responded with a smile as she shook off the melancholy from a few moments earlier.

She thought she should be concentrating on staying alive and free, not whether Michael would want her after she was safe. She needed to be safe in order for them to even have a chance.

They dressed in easy silence. She was beginning to feel less and less vulnerable around Michael. I'm beginning to feel, she thought. Why didn't she notice that before? Feelings were always fleeting for her, and she never focused on how she felt, instead focusing on what she thought. When she heard others talk about their feelings, she never could quite understand what they meant, but she was beginning to get the picture now. Michael was causing her to feel all sorts of ways: afraid, vulnerable, cherished, happy. He was bringing her out of her head. She couldn't believe it took having a man in her life before she could get in touch with this part of herself.

"Ready to eat?" Michael asked, walking to the door.

She followed behind him, her eyes smiling. Michael smiled back as they made their way down the hallway and into the lobby. Steve, Rob, and Tony were already waiting on them.

"How late are we?" Michael asked his brothers.

"We just got here ourselves," Tony replied with a knowing grin.

It was at times like this he most thought about the brother they had lost in battle, Leroy. He recalled Rob placing a plastic MRE bag over Leroy's exposed intestine and then wrapping it with tape from his first-aid kit.

"It'll be alright. You're going to be fine," Michael lied to Leroy, wishing to see anything but death in his eyes.

Leroy had coughed up blood and it dribbled down his chin as he tried to ask Michael to deliver his goodbye letter to his wife Kristen. They all carried letters to be delivered to their loved ones should they die on the field, and it was a brother's responsibility to ensure the letter reached the designee.

Michael remembered the look of devastation in Kristen's eyes as he walked up to her door. She had already been told about her husband's death, but she had known the hardest part, hearing his last words to her, had yet to come. She had reached out her hand and took the dirty envelope from Michael.

"Stay with me," she'd pleaded as she pushed the door open for Michael to enter her home.

When Michael stepped inside, she's motioned for him to sit on the couch. To his surprise, she'd sat next to him, needing the human contact. She'd opened the letter and started to read it, sobbing, tears streaming down her face.

Handing the letter to Michael, she'd pleaded, "Read it to me."

Michael couldn't deny his brother's wife's request. He'd read the letter but couldn't keep the tears from filling his own eyes. After he'd finished reading Leroy's last words to Kristen, they'd sat holding each other. Kristen had lost the love of her life, and Michael had lost one of his best friends, his brother.

"There's a diner across the street. Is that okay with everyone?" Tony asked, looking at Emma for a response. He knew the guys would eat anything after those MREs they had eaten for days and days on end.

"Anything works for me," Emma replied, not picky about where they ate just as long as they did so soon.

"All right then, let's hit the road," Tony said, turning to the door.

They followed Tony across the street and into the diner. Five minutes later they were seated with fresh cups of coffee.

Tony spoke first. "Emma, we have a damn good plan. It will work. Your safety is our number one priority."

She looked at Michael and plastered a smile onto her face. Michael noticed her smile didn't reach her eyes. Emma was afraid, but she wouldn't show these men her fear. She would be brave, and tough, and trust in them to protect her.

It made Tony's heart feel good that his brother had found a woman who could take away his pain, even if for a moment. Michael was really quite changed from the serious, straight shooting man he knew. In combat, Michael was a machine. Michael was smiling more now than he'd smiled in the six years he'd known him. It was almost like he could breathe again, and that made Tony damn protective of the woman who brought about such a change in his brother.

Tony would never admit it to anyone, but he saw the same signs of stress in Michael he had seen in himself. Tony knew if anything were to happen to Emma, Michael would lose the hard fought control he had been clinging to after combat. Combat did that to a man. It changed the fundamental nature of who he was. Tony knew Michael fought for control every day after leaving the military. He knew because he himself was fighting the same battle. No, Tony wouldn't let anything happen to Michael's Emma, and it was the deep love he felt for his brother that caused him to feel so deeply for this woman he did not know.

"What can I get you to eat?" the waitress said, grinning at Tony.

They ordered their food and when it came, they all ate in silence. Emma couldn't finish her large breakfast of eggs, hash browns, pancakes, and sausage, but the guys had no trouble.

"Glad to see you have an appetite, Emma," Steve said, shoveling the last bite into his mouth.

"I can always eat," Emma replied, smiling at Steve. It was strange, but she didn't feel self-conscious in front of these men. She could get used to the feeling of comfort she felt around them.

They finished with their coffee. "I got this," Tony said. When the waitress came back with the receipt, she made sure to give Tony a smile and wink before leaving the table. They all stood and put on their coats. Then they made their way back to the hotel.

"Grab your gear and meet in our room in fifteen minutes," Michael said to his brothers as he led Emma, with a hand on the small of her back, to the elevator.

Once inside the room, Michael pulled Emma closer to him and kissed her long and hard on the lips. She moaned into his mouth, parting her lips to allow his tongue room to taste her. He couldn't let himself think this might be the last time he would kiss her. He poured his soul into the kiss, deepening it. He tangled his hand into her hair and pulled her closer to him, her breasts molding to his hard chest.

Emma's fingers traced the V of his back as her heart beat feverishly against her chest. They embraced each other until there was a knock at the door.

Michael regretfully pulled away from her warm, soft flesh.

Emma was breathing hard, and she unconsciously placed her fingers against her kiss-swollen lips, remembering the exquisite kiss as she stared absently into space. She was taken by this man, and there was nothing she wanted more in the world than to remember exactly the way that kiss had felt for the rest of her life.

Michael opened the door, and his brothers walked into the room, making it feel very small. "Ready to do this?" Tony grinned at Michael after noticing Emma's trance-like state.

"You do that to her," Tony whispered for Michael's ears only.

Michael smiled at his brother and then looked at his Emma.

"Emma, baby? Are you ready to do this?" Michael asked her in a gentle voice. He knew she was frightened. Hell, he was frightened, too.

"Huh, what?" Emma mumbled, coming back into her head.

"I said, are you ready?" Michael asked, feeling better than he had ever remembered at the thought of having such an effect on her.

Truth be told, he remembered every moment they had spent together. He remembered the way her body arched under his when he was driving into her, her soft moans, and her dirty words spoken only for him. He remembered the way she climaxed around his cock. He remembered the way his cock felt sheathed by her mouth. He could feel himself pressing against his jeans. He better stop remembering and get down to business.

He grabbed his bags and headed towards the door. The men, plus one beautifully delicate Emma, made their way to the cars. They loaded their gear into the trunks and started their three-hour drive to kidnap Ahmed.

CLOSER

Outside of Pittsburgh, the men stopped to acquire a windowless van parked beside a garage. They cleaned it out, leaving all of the painting materials in the driveway. It was easy enough to get into, hotwire, and remove before anyone could become the wiser.

Steve, Tony, and Rob stowed away in the back of the van dressed in civilian combat gear: jeans, boots, and coats with bullet-proof vests underneath. Michael drove with Emma in the passenger seat. The directions Ahmed had sent ordered for Emma to be dropped off at Warehouse P7 in Highland Park. They found it in the middle of several abandoned warehouses. The garage door was open, waiting for Michael's delivery.

Michael pulled up to the garage door where a man stopped him. Michael assumed he was security for Ahmed. With a thick Algerian accent, the man asked, "What you doing here?"

Michael said, "Let me pull a little inside, and then I can deliver the package to Ahmed."

This was apparently good enough, as the man allowed Michael to pull ten feet into the warehouse. Michael could see Ahmed a good twenty feet away, standing next to a rather unremarkable dark van. He wore a ponytail of straggly hair. His jeans were dirty and full of holes, and his blue windbreaker was doing nothing to keep him warm.

If this went down wrong, he would never find Emma. But he couldn't think like that. Michael took a deep breath to clear his mind. He pulled to a stop, the security guard's gun trained on him. The guard peered into the van, trying to see behind him. The guard kept glancing back at Emma as if the sight of her made him mad. He would definitely hurt Emma. Michael had to work fast to keep the others' positions in the van a secret.

Michael reached behind him to pull out his wallet to prove his identity but instead pulled out his 9mm Beretta with a silencer and shot the unsuspecting security guard. With a clean shot between the eyes, the guard dropped to the ground. Ahmed saw this and started to run.

Upon the sound of gunfire, Emma jumped in her seat while Rob, Steve, and Tony jumped out of the back doors of the van and took off running after Ahmed. Tony held out the taser in front of him and pointed it at Ahmed. He only had to be within twenty feet of the man and the taser would fire, sinking its hooks into the man's skin, rendering him incapacitated for five seconds. As Tony neared the man, he pulled the trigger, firing the taser. Its needle barbs went straight through Ahmed's wind breaker and into his skin. Ahmed dropped to the ground, unmoving. Before Tony and Rob could reach him, Ahmed was on his feet and running again with the needle barbs still attached to his skin. Tony pulled the trigger of the taser again, and again Ahmed dropped to the ground incapacitated. This time Rob was there and had him cuffed with a zip tie in under five seconds. Once Ahmed could move again, they helped him to his feet. Now the fun would start.

Tony ran back to pull the garage door closed while Steve and Rob watched Ahmed impatiently. On the way back, Tony stopped at the van and pulled out a black duffle bag full of tools. Michael kept his gun focused on Ahmed the entire time. Steve shoved Ahmed forcefully into a chair as Tony opened the bag and started dragging out tools. Ahmed looked over at Tony and sweat started to bead on his forehead. They could smell him. He smelled like he hadn't showered in weeks.

Maybe cracking Ahmed would be easy, Michael thought.

All the banter and good nature disappeared from the men. They were now soldiers, serious and deadly. Emma could see how they worked together as a close-knit team in times of war. They frightened her. Once Tony returned to Ahmed, Michael led Emma to the van.

"Get in the back of the van and don't look. Promise me you won't look," he pleaded with Emma. "I want you to wear these headphones. Listen to my iPod for a while," he cajoled.

"You're going to hurt him, aren't you?" Emma whispered.

Michael couldn't meet Emma's eyes. He did not want her to know this side of him, but he wouldn't lie to her. He nodded his head.

"Are you going to kill him, Michael?" Emma questioned him, meeting his eyes for the first time since they pulled into the warehouse.

"No, Emma. I'm not going to kill him. But I can guarantee you I'm going to make sure he wishes he were dead," he snarled, psyching himself up for what had to be done.

Emma flinched. This side of Michael scared her. Although she had only known Michael a short time, she trusted her gut, and her gut said Michael would never hurt her. But she would have to give some thought to being with someone who wouldn't think twice about hurting someone else, even if he was the bad guy. Would she do the same thing if she were in Michael's shoes? If her mom or dad or even Michael were the one to be taken, would she not do everything in her power to get them back? Would she not hurt people to get information to save the ones she loved?

She thought about that for a second. As if a light bulb lit up, she realized she truly loved Michael. She knew that hurting the dirty man would be Michael's last resort. He wouldn't just start torturing him, would he? She really didn't know Michael, and yet she had fallen for him. The realization had taken her aback. It was too soon. Her head worked to convince her heart that it was just the adrenaline and danger of the situation that had hyped up these feelings she'd never felt before. What would she do if something happened

144

to Michael? The mere thought made tears stream down her cheeks. So she sat in the back of the van with the realization of her love for Michael at the forefront of her mind. She cried for what Michael had to do. She cried for who Michael had to be. She cried for what the bad man was going to endure to keep his secrets.

She knew in her heart that Michael didn't like hurting people and that it probably caused him a great deal of guilt. Michael was very caring when it came to her well-being. He couldn't be that caring and be a monster at the same time. No, the things Michael did weighed heavily upon him. She noticed his guilt in the lines around his eyes. She noticed his guilt buried in the depth of his soul when he looked at her. She made up her mind. From now on, she would be a rock Michael could lean on when the things he had seen and done were too much for him to endure. She loved him.

In her mind, a rational voice spoke up again. *"What if he doesn't want you there for him?"* She cried some more.

Michael left her and walked back to Ahmed. Rob wasn't wasting any time with the questioning. "Where is she? Where are you holding the American woman?" Rob demanded, grabbing the collar of Ahmed's windbreaker.

He pulled the man by the collar. Ahmed could feel the spit land on his face as Rob made demands for answers that Ahmed wouldn't give. Of course, Ahmed knew where the terrorist cell was holding the American woman. He had just come from there. But telling that to these men would get his family killed. He had a wife and kids to think about, not to mention he was a true martyr for his cause. He would endure their torture, their questions, to save his wife and family, to save the plan to take down the American government.

Tony pulled out a pair of pliers and approached Ahmed, making a show of the tool he had in his hand. Sweat dripped from Ahmed's head and onto his worn windbreaker. Was Ahmed strong enough to endure their torture? He kept telling himself he had to be. Then he heard a scream and realized it was coming from his own mouth. Tony had removed this thumbnail with the pliers. The pain was intense and brought immediate tears to Ahmed's eyes.

Ahmed had lived a relatively calm life before joining the GIA. He was actually recruited for his knowledge of weaponry. He heard the screaming again and begged the big man to stop.

"Please, no more. No more," he sobbed through agony.

"We can be done if you tell us where they are holding the American woman," Tony said with deadly control.

The blood that was dripping from Ahmed's fingers formed a little puddle on the concrete floor. Ahmed knew he wouldn't bleed to death. He just had to be stronger than they were. He wanted to see America get what it had coming to it, and the GIA was just the nefarious organization with the underground power to deliver justice.

Emma could hear the man screaming even through the earbuds. Whatever they were doing was causing him a great deal of pain. Surely he couldn't stand much more. Then the wretched sound ripped from his body again. She cried and turned the headphones up louder.

Five of his ten fingernails were gone. Losing a fingernail caused one of the worst pains a human body could bear because of the exposed nerve endings. Ahmed had never experienced this type of intense, relentless pain before. He wasn't sure he could endure that same torture inflicted upon his other hand.

"Once I remove all of your fingernails, I'll start removing the tips of your fingers," Michael said to Ahmed. "Is the American woman still alive?" Rob's face fell at Michael's question, but it had to be asked. She could already be dead and then their whole plan would have to change.

"She's alive," Ahmed sobbed. "She's hurt, but she's alive. Please, I can't tell you anymore. They will kill my family," he reasoned as tears cleansed a path down his dirty face.

Rob gave silent thanks that they hadn't killed her yet. She was strong, and as long as she was alive, she would be all right.

"You should have thought about that before joining such a ruthless terrorist organization," Steve responded, walking closer to Ahmed. This time it was Steve who picked up the pliers. He reached down and clasped them together tight against Ahmed's nail. He twisted, keeping his tight grip. The fingernail peeled off, and Ahmed passed out. The pool of blood on the concrete floor was growing larger by the second. Tony got the smelling salts from his bag. He walked over and held the salts under Ahmed's nose, bringing the man back from his reprieve.

"We still have four more fingers to go before we start cutting," Michael suggested to Ahmed.

"Please, no more," he begged.

"Then tell us what we want to know," Rob responded.

"She is being held at a house in Homestead about twenty minutes north of here," he heaved, trying to catch his breath.

"You are going to show us," Michael commanded as he got bandages for Ahmed's fingernail beds.

Rob took care to bandage Ahmed up so he wouldn't lose any more blood. Once Rob was finished and Tony had finished packing up the tools, Michael did a little reconnaissance to make sure they'd left no traces in the warehouse. Michael motioned for the guys to wait a few minutes before bringing Ahmed to the van. Michael opened its back door to find Emma's beautiful face stained with tears.

He crawled into the van and sat next to her, burying her face in his chest. "You could still hear him, couldn't you?" he asked as he stroked her hair, keeping her tight against his chest. He couldn't bear to look into her eyes while she was crying. It would kill what was left of his soul. He rocked her back and forth.

"Did he tell you where Lizzie is?" she sobbed between breaths.

"Yes. And it wasn't as bad as it could have been. He still has all of his fingers," he joked, trying to

148

lighten the mood. But it wasn't funny. She clung tighter to him as he rocked her gently back and forth.

"He's going to show us where to find her. Score one for the good guys today," he said, trying in vain to make himself feel better despite the torture he'd just inflicted upon another human being.

After hearing the guilt in his voice, she hugged him even closer.

"What can I do to make it better, Emma?" he gently asked her, coaxing her chin up so he could meet her eyes.

He knew what he would find in her expression would rip him apart, but he would take it like a man. When their eyes meet, he was floored at the love which shined through. Emma looked at him with love and understanding. He thumbed the teardrop that spilled down her cheek and kissed the spot it left. He kissed her eyelids, her nose, her forehead, and then he brought his mouth to her lips.

She melted into the kiss. It was exactly what she needed to heal her aching heart.

"We better get moving. Rob is anxious to find Lizzie," he said as he pulled reluctantly from her embrace.

"I understand," was all that she could mutter as she crouched and moved into the passenger seat of the van.

It took the better part of the day to get the information they needed. The men loaded the van with their tools and Ahmed. They had to recover their cars. Once that was accomplished, they found a Best

Western to hole up in for the night. Emma needed time to recover. Hell, Michael needed time to recover.

They pulled into the parking lot with a very anxious Rob. Michael asked for a room on the first floor next to the emergency exit again and was given the key. They snuck Ahmed in through the emergency exit and into Rob's room. If they weren't going in tonight, Rob wanted that fucker Ahmed right where he could keep his eye on him. No chance of a phone call alerting his terrorist friends to what went down. Rob did, however, need Ahmed to make a phone call saying his employee, Michael, was delayed by a day due to weather and would not be delivering the package until tomorrow. Rob had to make sure Lizzie stayed safe. But Rob knew if he and his brothers didn't save Lizzie, the terrorists would surely kill her, with or without the package. Rob wanted to go in, guns blazing. He had to calm down and listen to reason before he was able to agree to develop a plan to retrieve Lizzie. Michael had said that they needed to treat this like any other hostage retrieval they had done, and Rob knew he was right.

"Ahmed, write down the address of the house," Rob demanded as he shoved a piece of paper and pen in his face.

"What you need this for? I told you, I show you," Ahmed said with a worried expression.

"Just do it," responded Rob, standing there with the paper and pen in his outstretched hand. Ahmed reluctantly took the paper and wrote down the address of the house. "Now, I need you to make a phone call delaying your arrival by a day. Blame it on the weather," he said, handing Ahmed the phone. "And don't try alerting your friends to anything, or I will kill you right here, right now," Rob growled.

Ahmed did as he was instructed. Rob felt a little better about having time to come up with a plan now, for as far as the terrorist cell knew, Michael would still deliver Emma tomorrow. And Rob couldn't help but think about the real danger Emma put herself in by even going along with this mission. Things could go wrong, and she could end up like his Lizzie, held prisoner by the bad guys.

CLOSER

CHAPTER
FOURTEEN

All of the brothers had gathered in Rob's room to begin working on a plan to retrieve Lizzie. Before conversation could get underway, Rob's phone started buzzing with an incoming call. Rob looked at the phone and then at his brothers.

"Who is it?" Michael asked as he watched Rob's worried expression morph into one of anguish.

"It's the GIA," Rob explained, pressing the green button on his cell phone and bringing it to his ear. "Hello," Rob said cautiously. He knew pissing these people off would get his Lizzie killed. The phone was silent for a minute before the same man that contacted him previously started to speak.

"Right now, my man has his cock buried deep in your girlfriend," the man enjoyed saying as Rob dropped to his knees, tears spilling from his eyes.

The brothers stood around Rob, looking like they were ready to kill someone.

"What more can I do?" Rob asked the man on the phone.

"He will leave her, once he's done of course, if you deliver Emma, her field notes, and the prototype to us within two days. If you fail to meet my requirements, I will turn my beast loose on your American woman again," the man said while Rob raked a hand through his hair.

"Let me talk to her. How do I know she is still alive?" Rob asked, begging for a chance to hear his name whispered on her lips.

"You want to hear her moan, you got it," the man smiled through the phone.

Rob could hear her grunting and screaming as the terrorist raped her.

"Leave her alone! I swear to God I am going to take great pleasure in making you feel nothing but pain before I kill you, you mother fucker," Rob countered in a deadly calm voice. Something came over Rob. Michael could see it. Rob had stopped crying and he stood up.

"Now you listen to me, you sick sonofabitch, I will bring everything you require in three days' time. I will meet up with my man and personally deliver Emma Welby myself. But so you know, I will be walking out of there with Lizzie after I have taken great pleasure in killing you and everyone else in your little group," he calmly told the man on the phone.

Lizzie screamed in the background again and Rob went deathly pale.

"I need three days to drive back up to Maine and then back to you again. Where will I make the drop?" Rob questioned, not giving away the fact that they had their exact location from Ahmed.

"I will call you in three days. I expect you will be back in Pittsburgh at that time with everything I require. I will provide instructions to you then," the man said in a calm, happy voice. And why shouldn't he feel happy? He thought Rob was playing right into his hands. Little did he know Rob wasn't alone, or that Rob wasn't kidding when he said he would be the one to kill him.

Michael made his way back to the room he shared with Emma after formulating a plan to retrieve Lizzie. It was already 2200 hours. It took a long time to calm Rob down and to reassure him waiting was the best course of action. There was also the little matter of retrieving all of the field notes Emma had complied on Project Hummingbird, as well as sneaking the prototype out of the lab.

Michael raked his hand over his stubbly face as he made his way down the hall to his room. He slid the keycard into the door and viewed the green light. He pushed the door open and saw Emma sitting on the double bed, staring off into space. He knew it had been a long, tiring day for her. A tiring couple of days, by his count, and it was nowhere near over yet. He walked into the room and stood beside the bed. "I just want to hold you tonight. I need to reassure myself you're safe," Michael told Emma as he ran the back of his hand down her cheek.

She met his gaze and smiled. She scooted over and made a place for him to sit down beside her.

"How are you feeling?" he asked her, running his fingers up and down her arm.

"Much better. I am not as sore as I was yesterday," she explained.

He lifted her shirt to look at the bruises, which were now a dark shade of purple. He ran his fingers slowly over each bruise, and she winced. He knew he should just hold her tonight. Her body was still recovering, and he couldn't take the chance of hurting her again. The skin around her eyes had started to turn the same shade purple. He bent his head forward and lightly kissed under each eye. He ran his lips lightly over her face down to her mouth. Her busted lip was closing nicely. She would be just fine from the injuries she suffered at Ingrams' hands. He just had to take extra care with her.

She craved his touch like a drought craved rain. She needed to feel his body pressed against hers to know she was indeed safe. She leaned into his touch, reaching out with her own hand to cup his stubbly jaw. She ran her thumb over his bottom lip, imagining his sweet taste.

The stubble on his jaw made him look rougher, sexier. Would he take her again, make her forget herself and the situation? Would he press into her core with his perfect thick cock and force naughty words out of her mouth again? God, she hoped so.

He had left her alone with her thoughts for a few hours, and in those hours her mind started wandering. She realized, after the adrenaline had subsided, that she was frightened at what was about to come. They still had to use her as bait to lure out the terrorist cell.

"Why can't we call Homeland Security and give them the address?" she questioned Michael as he sat next to her on the bed.

"Rob received a phone call from the terrorist cell while we were working on a plan," he said to her.

Emma sat up straight. "What did they say?" she asked with bated breath.

Michael told her of the new requirements. He explained how they would have to sneak out her field notes and prototype in order to save Lizzie. Her eyes glistened and tears streamed down her face. She was so sick of crying. She didn't want to feel so hopeless and so selfish at the same time. She allowed her work to define her for the past two years. Now she had to give it up to save someone's life. Not to be misunderstood, she told Michael she would gladly retrieve every last bit of information to save Lizzie. But she couldn't help but wonder what that meant for her identity. If she wasn't the one to develop and complete Project Hummingbird, then who was she?

"What if we get Homeland Security involved? Can't they help?" she begged Michael.

"Emma, I know that sounds easy, but remember someone with knowledge of your project gave it to a man who was supposed to kill you. We don't know who we can trust, and because of that, we trust no one," he assured her. "I am not going to let anything happen to you ever again. And that means we do this on our own. You can trust my brothers. I've known them for six years. We have been in some serious shit together and have always had each other's backs. They will protect you with their dying breath. The same way I will protect Lizzie with mine," he continued to explain as she looked into his deep, sincere eyes.

He would die for Lizzie, the same way he would die for her. She knew he would. Her gut refused to allow her head to argue.

She scooted down on the bed until she was lying down, staring up at the ceiling with new worries to think about.

"Get undressed," he commanded because he didn't want anything between them tonight. Tonight was about reassuring her she was his—his to protect and his to love. She crawled off the bed and watched his eyes as she slowly undressed for him. Knowing he was getting turned on watching her do something as simple as undress was a powerful feeling. She moved on her hands and knees, back to the lying position she had been in before ridding herself of her clothing. It was Michael's turn. He stood and locked eyes with hers as he removed his shirt. She stared unabashedly at his body. He removed his pants and his underwear while she appreciated his true beauty.

"You're the beautiful one, Michael," she boldly stated as he climbed into bed beside her. He pulled the covers over their bodies.

"Roll over. I want to feel that ass pressed against me tonight," he said to her as she complied and rolled onto her side.

She backed up against him until she felt his firm chest against her back, until she felt his stiff erection against her buttocks. He ran his fingers up and down her thigh before bringing his arm to cuddle around her middle.

Michael pulled her closer, still careful of her bruises. He tucked her head under his chin and inhaled her earthy, lavender scent, which calmed and relaxed him until he drifted off into sweet dreamland with her safely in his arms.

CLOSER

The curtains were drawn tight, keeping the sunlight from peering into the room. With a smile, she wriggled her hips against Michael's semi-hard erection. Michael opened his eyes and found her in the exact same position as the previous night.

"Good morning," he said sleepily into her hair.

"Good morning, yourself," she responded, pressing her ass up against his now hard member.

He ran his hand up to touch her breast. A moan escaped her smiling lips. She wanted him now. She didn't want to wait, because waiting was the worst possible thing they could do with each other right now. Who knew what the future held? Would she even be alive at this time tomorrow? No, she had to seize the day as it came. She was liking this newfound freedom, and she owed it all to the man who held her in a protective cocoon.

Michael continued rolling her nipple, tugging it lightly with his fingertips while he nibbled at the back of her neck. A zing of tingles made their way through her body, igniting her core. She instantly felt herself moisten as he continued to bite and then kiss the back of her neck. She especially liked the way his hot breath felt against her bare body. He rolled her over and braced himself on top of her. He lowered his head and pulled a taut nipple into his mouth. He sucked at her breast, causing her back to arch under his ministrations. She ran her hands down to his stiff cock and began stroking it. He moved to her other breast, paying it the same attention. While he sucked, she fisted his member. She was so wet from the attention her breasts were getting. She never knew it could feel so good.

"I need to get a condom," Michael told her.

"I'm on the pill," was all she said, expecting him to know that she trusted him with her life. She definitely didn't want him to move from his current position.

He lay on his side and she rolled over. He pulled her back against his chest. She lifted her leg and placed it on his. He took full advantage of the new position as his cock fell against her opening. He grabbed ahold of her hip and gently thrust his hips forward, entering her warm, dripping core from behind. They both moaned at the feeling of his thick cock entering her. The way her body responded to his, dripping wet at the smallest of touches, would never cease to amaze him.

He continued rocking his hips back and forth against her ass as he rubbed her clit. He pinched her nipple hard, and pain quickly dissolved to pleasure that shot through her body as he slammed into her core. She felt a renewed sense of arousal. She began to move her hips in rhythm with his, pushing her ass back as he thrust his cock forward.

Michael was going to take his time this morning. He pinched her nipple again before trailing his fingers back down to find her clit. He rubbed her as she began to buck wildly against his hips. He knew she was close so he increased his pressure and thrust into her harder and quicker. She screamed out his name as he pressed her clit hard, allowing her to ride out her orgasm on his cock. He loved the way her pussy clenched him when she came. It was enough to be his undoing, but not this morning.

"Get on your knees," he commanded.

He did what he'd been dying to do since he met her. He grabbed ahold of her hips and thrust deeply into her body, pulling her hips back against his forward thrust. He thrust into her again and again, bringing himself closer and closer to his own climax. Emma rose, her back against his chest, and wrapped her arm around his neck. She turned her face so he could capture her mouth as he continued rocking in and out of her body. He deepened the kiss as he moved his hand down to her clit. He began rubbing it with his fingers as he swallowed her moan. She shattered, exploding into the universe around his throbbing, aching cock. With one more thrust his body went tense, and he emptied himself into her. With each beat of his heart, he squirted his hot liquid deep into her core until it was running down her inner thigh. He ran his lips up and down her back before pulling out of her.

"Stay there, and I'll clean you up," he said, walking into the bathroom.

She heard the faucet turn on and then off. He returned with a warm washcloth and gently cleaned the cum that had dripped between her thighs.

"Are you hungry?" he asked, bending over to kiss her.

"I'm famished," she responded, looking at the clock.

"Let's get showers and then find the guys," he said, caressing her face.

Michael steadied himself, content in the knowledge he would have her again. Right now he had to get down to business. They showered together, keeping the touching and caressing to a minimum. He dried them both off. They found clothes and dressed without words.

He picked up the phone and dialed Rob's room.

"Ready to eat?" he asked Rob when he answered the phone. "Okay, see you in fifteen."

CHAPTER SIXTEEN

They made their way into the coffee shop that the desk clerk recommended for breakfast. This time Emma ate every last bite that was on her plate. She probably could have eaten more but didn't want to make herself sick. They made small talk, but all eyes were focused on Rob. He wasn't doing so well.

"What did you hear last night, man? Were they hurting Lizzie?" Michael asked as Rob met his gaze with sadness and determination.

"They raped her, man, while I was on the phone," Rob confessed. He never kept anything from these guys.

"Oh God," Emma gasped, covering her mouth with her hand in shock. Emma remembered how it felt to be violated. Ingrams had touched her despite her will and strength to resist him. She couldn't imagine what would have happened to her if Michael hadn't have found her.

What kind of monsters were they dealing with? She was now more determined than ever to get her notes and the prototype past security to save Lizzie.

"She's strong, ya know?" Rob said more to himself than the group. "She will make it through this.

I just hope we can get to her before they do it again," he said as his face turned a slight green color. He could feel the bile rising in his throat at the thought of what Lizzie was enduring. "I want them dead. No one survives," Rob assured himself as he spoke aloud to the group. "We go in, mow down those motherfuckers, and get Lizzie," he said, determination glinting in his eyes.

"We'll get her, Rob. I promise. We've got your back. It's just going to take time putting everything together, and we still have to make sure nothing happens to Emma," Michael said.

"Emma's here. She's fine. We aren't going to let anything happen to her," Rob hissed, "but Lizzie, she's in trouble, man. We have to go and get her. I am sick and tired of waiting."

"So we go back to Maine. We'll drive straight through and grab Emma's field notes and prototype, because regardless of who they have, we still have to protect this country. We get the stuff, stash it somewhere safe, and then get Lizzie. Two days max," Michael assured his best friend.

"I know you're right. I just can't think logically or rationally. I could hear her, man. I could hear what they were doing to her," he blurted as he cast his eyes down so no one would see him cry.

Emma wrapped an arm around Rob's shoulders.

"Look, I know I'm here and not in any immediate danger. I just want to say thank you for coming to my rescue. And I want you to know, I will be there when

166

we rescue Lizzie," she said, gently squeezing his shoulders.

"You can't be there, Emma," Michael cautioned.

"Like hell I can't. This directly relates to me. You said yourself you won't let anything happen to me. So don't. But I want to be there for Lizzie," she challenged, rubbing Rob's arm up and down in a reassuring manner.

"He's right, Emma," Rob said. "It's too dangerous for you. This whole thing could end up upside down, and you could be sitting there, held prisoner, right along with Lizzie," Rob continued, forcing back the tears.

"This is not open for debate, gentlemen," Emma concluded. "I'm going. I will be there for Lizzie. She's going to need a woman to look after her. I'll stay out of the way. Hell, give me a gun if you have to. I want to shoot them myself," she said, smiling, hoping to lighten the gravity of the situation.

"Do you even know how to use a gun?" Rob questioned, raising his eyebrows in speculation.

"As a matter of fact, my father is a big gun buff, so I grew up around them. I have shot everything from a 22 to a 457," she stated matter-of-factly.

"Fine, you want to go, you go. But you go in armed, and you stay the hell out of the way. If anyone comes at you, any one at all, you shoot first and ask questions later," Michael stuttered through the words stuck in his throat.

He couldn't believe he was agreeing to this. She was his to protect. He would just have to keep her by his side at all times. It probably was safer to be by his side than to be left in a car or hotel room somewhere. Just then, a gnawing started at the back of his throat. He felt the pit in his stomach grow. He was getting one of his famous gut feelings, and this one was screaming at him that this whole situation was going to end badly.

They paid their checks and got to their feet, slipping on their coats before heading to their cars. They were already packed and had checked out of the Best Western. Now they had the long, thirteen hour drive back to Emma's lab.

They arrived in Lewiston around 2100 hours. It was already dark, and everyone who worked at the lab had all gone for the evening. Emma hadn't been to work in a few days and had to come up with a viable reason quickly. She knew Paul would be expecting one.

"I'll tell Paul that I've been sick but am feeling better now, and that I need to get back to work on the project," Emma said to the men as they stood huddled in a circle a few blocks down from her office building. "I just don't know how I'm going to sneak everything out. That's the whole reason we have to leave our belongings at the security desk."

"How long has Paul been working here?" Michael asked.

"Longer than I have, and I've been here for three years," Emma explained, shivering against the biting cold. How these men were unaffected by the weather was a mystery to her.

"Then he trusts you, right?" Steve ventured.

"Yes, I suppose he does."

"That's good. We'll use that trust to get everything out. How many notebooks do you have?" Michael asked.

"Three spiral notebooks, plus two full mini-cassette tapes."

"How big is the Hummingbird?" Michael asked.

"It can fit into my palm," she said through chattering teeth.

"Okay, so here is what you're going to do. You stuff the notebooks in the back of your pants here," he said pulling on the back waist of her jeans. "You put the cassette tapes in your front pockets, and you keep the Hummingbird in the palm of your left hand," Michael continued.

"But won't Paul notice?" she doubtfully asked.

"He won't be looking for anything suspicious because he trusts you. We have to use that trust," Michael explained, rubbing Emma's shoulders.

"What if I give it away?" she asked. "What if I get nervous, choke, and expose the notebooks or worse, drop the Hummingbird?" she asked Michael with fear in her eyes.

"You won't. Just remember the reasons you're doing this. Someone wants what you know. We have to make sure that knowledge disappears, and we save Lizzie in the process." Michael quickly kissed her. "Now get a move on, and don't let anything stop you," Michael said with a smile as he spanked her rear. She smiled back even though this was a precarious situation.

She approached Paul at the security desk like she did every day for the last three years. She asked about his family and made small talk while she handed over her phone and purse to be put in lockup.

She explained away her absence and Paul said, "I hope you're feeling better, Emma."

"I'm starting to. Thank you, Paul," she said as she made her way to the stairs, not wanting anything to appear out of the ordinary.

After an hour's time, to keep Paul from becoming suspicious, she gathered her notebooks and placed them in the back of her pants, hiding the tops of the notebooks under her shirt. She stuffed the two cassette tapes into her jean's pockets and firmly wrapped her left fingers around the Hummingbird. She took the stairs back down to the security desk and tried her best to remain nonchalant. She took her purse and cell phone from him, struggling to place her cell phone in her purse with one hand. She smiled at Paul and made her way causally to the front doors.

As soon as she was outside, she began walking quickly the few blocks to reach the men. She had highly classified information with her and could not afford to be stopped or confronted. She rounded the corner and saw the men waiting exactly where she left them.

"I did it," she beamed proudly at them.

Before they could respond, a black van, much like the one waiting in the warehouse, pulled up beside her and two men jumped out. The men grabbed Emma and forced her into the already moving van.

Michael immediately rounded the car and got behind the wheel. As the van sped away, Michael and his brothers pursued. The van attempted to lose Michael several times with sharp turns, but Michael was able to keep up. He was not letting her out of his sight.

The van turned down an alleyway, and Michael made the same right turn. He chanced a look in his rearview mirror and saw his brothers were still behind him.

"Who is it?" Rob asked Michael as he held onto the dashboard while Michael increased his speed. The van sped away on a stretch of I-95 with Michael close behind.

"It's either the terrorists or the CIA. At this point, I have no fucking idea," Michael said as he closed the distance between his vehicle and the van.

The van got into the left lane with Michael right behind. The van moved into the middle lane in an attempt to outmaneuver Michael, but both cars in Michael's unit overtook the van, boxing it in from both sides. The van's driver began firing shots, busting out the passenger window. Rob ducked just in time. Michael slowed down a little so the driver couldn't get a clean shot.

Emma wasn't tied up, she'd just been thrown into the back of the moving vehicle. Perhaps she could reach up and put her arm around the driver's neck. She began to move, but the man in the back with her grabbed her ankle. Emma wiggled free and rammed her heel into the man's nose, causing him to cower in pain. She moved quickly behind the driver, reaching around his neck. She clenched her arm with all her might, locking it with her other arm, as the man pulled at her, trying to remove her chokehold. She didn't let go. No one was taking this information from her. She felt the other man pulling at her leg but didn't look back. The driver was starting to lose consciousness, the passenger forced to steer the van so they didn't lose control. The driver, in a last ditch effort, fired the gun under his arm and through the seat. The wheel jerked and the van spun and toppled over. It rolled twice before coming to rest on its side.

Michael, Rob, Steve, and Tony were at the side of the van the second it stopped moving. Tony pried the back of the door open to see Emma lying there on the side of the van, blood pooling around her body. The passenger grabbed all of the top secret materials from Emma, jumped out of the van, and took off down the street. Before the men could get to him, he had carjacked a vehicle and sped off down the highway. The men quickly decided that Emma took precedence. They carefully extricated her from the van and gently laid her down on the highway. Tony checked the driver, but he was dead on impact.

"He got away," Tony told Michael.

Michael couldn't hear, he couldn't see, he couldn't even think. His world stopped. He only knew one thing: his Emma had been shot.

"We have to get her back to your house, Rob!" he shouted.

"Let me in to see," Rob calmly insisted.

Michael was cradling Emma's lifeless body in his arms. Rob reached for Emma, but Michael shook his head back and forth through his tears. A heart-wrenching sob escaped Michael's throat. Rob knew his friend was losing it. He was close to losing it himself last night.

"I need to examine her, Michael. Give her to me," Rob demanded, reaching out to remove Emma from Michael's arms.

This time Michael let her go. Rob laid her back on the concrete and rolled her to her side.

"Look, an exit wound," he exclaimed to Michael.

Michael could taste the bile rise in the back of his throat. He was going to be sick. He stood and made his way to the other side of the van before he lost everything he had eaten in the last few hours. After retching, he came back to Emma a bit more focused than he had been just a few minutes ago.

"How bad? Give it to me straight," he demanded.

"She's going to make it. It's mainly a flesh wound, but I need to get her back to my house, *now*," Rob stated. Michael thanked God his Emma was going to be okay.

"How do you know she didn't damage any organs?" Michael asked Rob as he bent down to pick Emma's lifeless body up into his arms.

"I don't and I won't, not until we get back to my house. Put her in the back of my car," Rob commanded as he got in the driver's seat.

CLOSER

For the second time in so many days, Michael climbed into the backseat with an injured Emma, cradling her body against his chest.

CHAPTER
SEVENTEEN

They pulled onto Rob's street, and Michael got out of the car with Emma's unconscious body.

"Why isn't she awake?" he barked at Rob as he carried her to the house.

"Her body probably shut down from the pain. You remember how painful it is to be shot," Rob said.

Michael walked to the couch and laid his porcelain doll down. He went into the kitchen and came back with a dry dishcloth to stop the bleeding.

"Emma, baby. Wake up," he cajoled.

She was firmly in the land of darkness. She couldn't hear or feel. Michael kept firm pressure on her wound until Rob came into the room with his first-aid kit.

"I need in. I'm going to check her and then stitch her up," Rob told Michael as he moved in front of Emma's body. Rob poked and prodded. Still Emma remained unconscious. "It's better she's out, man. That way she won't feel anything," Rob reassured Michael.

Michael paced back and forth while Rob got out his suture kit.

"Think of it as a flesh wound. She is going to be fine. The bullet totally missed all of her organs. The only thing you will have to watch for is infection from the stitches," Rob said, trying to calm a very agitated Michael down. "Look. See how it just went through the extreme right side of her body," Rob told Michael as he pointed to her side.

"How long will she be out?" Michael asked worried about Emma's lack of consciousness.

"I hope she's out until I get her stitched up," Rob assured Michael in a calm voice.

"What can I do to help? I have never felt so helpless in my life," Michael pleaded with Rob.

"Just calm down and relax before I have to treat you for a heart attack," Rob said to his friend, trying to lighten the situation.

Rob was always extremely calm under pressure. They all were, but when Michael had seen Emma lying in a pool of her own blood, he lost it. He thought he lost everything. He had finally found the one woman to calm his ravaged soul and she had almost been taken away from him—twice.

"Will she need to go to the hospital?" Michael asked, furrowing his brows. He couldn't let her go to the hospital, not with so many different people after her. How would he keep her safe from the CIA agent if she was admitted to the hospital?

"No, I think after I get her stitched up and get her a shot for the pain, she should be just fine. She will be up and moving tonight, she just may be a little tender. So take it easy on her, eh?" Rob said to Michael, smiling at him with a knowing expression.

"The only thing I am going to be doing with her is taking care of her every need," Michael said, exasperated at the thought of her being shot.

He remembered the pain he felt when he was shot in the back. The bullet entered under his right shoulder blade. Thank God it was a through-and-through, but the pain was still intense. He didn't pass out, but he wasn't complaining when they shot him full of morphine to dull his senses. He had been able to get up and move around within a day, although it hurt like hell. He knew Rob knew his shit and wouldn't lie to him about Emma's condition. If Rob said they had to take her to the hospital, they would. Rob assured Michael she should wake when the pain subsided. She was damn lucky because this whole situation could have been a lot worse.

Michael watched in agony as Rob pulled the sutures through her skin with the U-shaped needle.

"I finished the front. I only needed to put five sutures in. Help me roll her onto her side so I can close the exit wound," Rob told Michael.

Michael and Rob carefully rolled Emma onto her side, placing her arms above her head so they were out of the way. It took Rob a few minutes. Thankfully she had been shot with a low caliber pistol.

"The bleeding has stopped. Let's let her rest on the couch until she wakes. Then we'll move her to the guest room," Rob said as Michael gently stroked the hair from her face.

"Lizzie, man. What the fuck are we going to do?" Rob asked as he ran a hand through his short hair in agitation. It was taking too long to get to her and the longer they waited, the more she had to endure. "They're not going to keep her alive forever. What if that was the terrorists who grabbed Emma? They have all of the information. Do they even need her now? What is it that will keep Lizzie alive?" Rob asked, pacing.

Michael hesitated, the words coming slowly from deep in his gut. He didn't want to have to say this to his best friend, but Rob needed to hear it. He had to start to prepare for the worst because if it was the terrorists, then Lizzie's chances of survival were slim.

"I know, man. If it was the terrorists, then I am not going to lie to you. It doesn't look good. If they don't need Emma, they don't need you. You know what that means for Lizzie," Michael said regretfully to his best friend.

"I can't lose her, man. I saw the way you reacted to finding Emma today. I know you have feelings for her. I'm in love with Lizzie, man. She's my life." He desperately looked around as if he just realized the horror of the situation.

Rob turned, tears streaming down his cheeks. It couldn't be too late. He had to remain positive, or he would lose his mind.

"Is the Hummingbird fully operational?" Rob asked Michael with hope in his heart.

"Emma said there was a flaw in the design, and it was that flaw that kept it from working."

"Then there is a chance they still need her to fix it," Rob said.

"It is certainly possible. Emma is the only one who knows how the Hummingbird works. It was her invention," Michael said, noticing Emma's fingers twitching in his hand. He looked down at her and saw her eyes were still closed.

Emma could hear voices, but she had trouble opening her eyes. God, did her right side hurt. She didn't know where she was or why she was in pain. She tried opening her eyes, but they were heavy like she was in a sound sleep, yet she could hear him—she could hear Michael. What was the last thing she remembered? She was trying to keep that asshole from shooting at Michael. She had her arm wrapped firmly around his neck and then nothing. She had no idea where she was. Still she just knew Michael was with her. That fact calmed her racing heart. She tried again to open her eyes but couldn't.

She heard Michael. "Emma, baby. Wake up. It's time to open your beautiful eyes. Come on Emma, let me see you."

She struggled to do as he asked. The light blinded her, and she quickly shut her eyes again.

"I saw her open her eyes!" Michael exclaimed to Rob. Rob approached and stood beside Michael on the couch. They both were staring expectantly at her face. "Come on, Emma. We need to talk to you," Michael whispered, hoping beyond hope she could hear him.

She did hear him, and she wanted to open her eyes, it was just that the light hurt.

"The light," she coughed with a dry throat.

How long had she been out of it she wondered? Michael got up and flipped the light switch, darkening the room. Sitting next to her, he brushed the hair from her face and took her hand in his. "I made it darker for you, baby. Come back to me. Open your eyes," Michael implored.

Emma opened her eyes, and the first thing she saw was his very worried expression. "What happened?" she asked Michael as she struggled parting her lips.

"We were hoping you could tell us," Michael said, smiling as he visibly deflated in front of her, releasing his held breath. She was awake and talking. Thank you, God, Michael prayed silently. "What's the last thing you remember?" Michael asked her, stroking her hand.

"Why does my side hurt so badly?" she asked as she tried to sit up.

Michael put a firm hand on her shoulder and kept her from rising. "You were shot." He groaned at the memory of her lifeless body.

"Where am I?" she continued, confused. She looked around a familiar living room. She noticed the mauve draperies hanging at the bay windows.

"You are at Rob's house. He stitched up the bullet holes those bastards put in you. Are you in a lot of pain?" He winced, hoping her answer would be *no*.

"It's not too bad, just a throbbing ache," she responded, hiding her true pain from him, knowing how he would react.

"Why did you try to overpower the driver?" Michael asked Emma.

"Because he was shooting at you," she said in all seriousness. "Plus, there was no way I was going to go again quietly," she said resolutely.

Michael admired her determination and courage. It hit him then—she risked her life for him. If he didn't love her before, he did now.

"The driver you had in a chokehold shot you through the seat of the van. The passenger got away with all of your notes and the prototype," he told her, waiting for her reaction. He knew how much this project meant to her.

"He got everything?" She moaned, devastated at the thought. "Who was it? Can we get it back?"

"We aren't sure who tried to take you." Michael hated telling her he didn't have an answer.

Tony walked into the room, relief evident in his eyes as he gazed at a very alert Emma. "I ran the tags on the van, but they came back stolen," Tony told the group in the living room. "Without a starting point, I don't have much to go on."

They already knew where the terrorist were holding Lizzie, so Ahmed would be of no further help until they got on the road. For all intents and purposes, they had hit a dead end.

"Emma, we're going to rescue Lizzie, and we want you to stay here with Tony and rest," Michael asserted as he bent forward to kiss her lips gently. "I can't risk anything else happening to you," he told her matter-of-factly.

He was going to have to come clean about what she meant to him, but that would have to wait. She was safe now, and he knew Tony would protect her.

Michael stood and asked if he could speak to Tony in the kitchen. Tony followed. Michael placed his hand on Tony's shoulder. "Tony, I know you wanted in on this mission, but I really need you here to watch over Emma. I can't do what I have to do if I am worried about her safety and other than Rob, you are the only one I would trust leaving her with," Michael insisted.

"I know what she means to you, man. It's written all over your face. In fact, I thought we were going to have to give you the morphine when she was shot," Tony said in his light-hearted manner. "Are you sure you, Rob, and Steve can handle this on your own?"

"We don't have a choice. People are after her. I doubt they know she is here at Rob's, but in case they do, I need you here, armed to the hilt, ready to shoot any motherfucker who tries to walk in that door," Michael said, pointing to the door off the kitchen.

"I got you, man. I'll keep her safe," Tony insisted, all kidding aside.

"Thank you. I will owe you for the rest of my life."

"Don't worry. You have my word, I will die before anything happens to your girl," Tony reassured Michael, holding out his hand.

Michael took Tony's hand in his and pulled him in for a one-armed hug.

182

Michael walked back into the living room and was surprised to see Emma sitting up. Her face was contorted in pain.

"Tony, you're going to have to make sure she rests," Michael said, smiling at Emma.

"I'll do my best." Tony winked at Emma. He admired her strength.

Emma really wanted to be there for Lizzie, but her current condition made that next to impossible. She would have to remain planted where she was if she hoped to recover quickly. She thought back to her actions in the van. She didn't know where she found the strength to kick that man in the face and bust his nose, nor would she ever understand how she managed to subdue the man driving. She was just thankful all of the men were safe and in one piece.

Emma couldn't help feeling despair over losing her life's work. She fought the feeling with everything she could because Lizzie was now the priority. She wouldn't allow her head to even think of losing the project forever. Michael would get it back. She had to have faith. Admitting that her project was gone forever was something she wouldn't even entertain because it would destroy her.

She had to remain strong for Michael and worry about his safety now. He would be infiltrating a terrorist cell. Didn't she hear that they usually booby-trapped their hold ups? She couldn't rest as long as Michael was out there in danger. Thank God he was out of the military, because she didn't think she could handle him constantly putting himself in danger. But what if that was what he wanted for himself once all this was over? What if he no longer wanted her? Her heart was already involved. Maybe, if she gave her head a chance, it could talk her heart out of loving him.

Emma wasn't sure what time it was when she awoke on the couch. "Michael," she whispered into the dark living room. She looked to the window in the front room and saw the full moon beaming back at her. Within a second, Michael was at her side.

"What is it, Emma? Do you need more pain medication?"

"Yes, I hurt. I also would feel better if I could lie down flat and not be propped up by so many pillows."

She looked at Michael's furrowed brows. She could tell he was worried about her. She needed to ease his worry so he could get some sleep. The next two days would be dangerous for him.

"Why don't we go to the bedroom Rob offered earlier, and you can sleep lying flat." Michael ran his hand through her hair, and she felt herself relaxing.

"Sounds good," she said slowly, trying again to hide her pain.

Michael would give anything to take away that pain she tried to hide. He hadn't been there to protect her. Instead, she had protected him. Michael scooped her into his arms and carried her up the stairs. Reaching the top step, he could hear Rob snoring. It surprised him that Rob could sleep with all of the stress he was under. He turned and walked to the guest bedroom. He set Emma on her feet and pulled down the covers for her. She gently sat on the edge of the bed and slowly turned. She laid herself down with a consternation of intense pain.

"I'll go get you that shot." Michael stood to leave her. "Rob. Wake up, man. I need another shot for Emma," Michael said, shaking his brother's shoulder roughly.

He hated to wake up Rob from his deep sleep, but he would do it for Emma. For Emma he would do anything. Rob trudged into the master bathroom and retrieved the syringe from his medical kit.

"Here. This will help her sleep through the night." He handed Michael the syringe filled with morphine.

Michael didn't even want to know where Rob got his pain medicines. He was just thankful he had them. Michael injected Emma's arm with the syringe.

Emma immediately felt the lessening of her pain. "Sleep with me." She patted the spot next her on the bed.

Michael walked around the bed and got under the covers. He pushed against her body and placed his right arm over her stomach, careful not to touch her wound. He placed his left arm under her neck to create a cocoon for her to sleep. Within minutes, her breathing slowed from labored breaths to a soft, steady rhythm. Confident in her newfound comfort, Michael allowed himself to drift off to sleep.

Michael awoke before Emma, watching her sleep. *How could he ever let her go?* He knew his brothers were waiting downstairs, anxious to start their mission. He carefully slid his arm from behind her neck and pressed a soft kiss to her forehead, getting out of bed without disturbing her.

Downstairs, Rob had coffee and breakfast ready to go for everyone. Michael sat down and accepted his plate of eggs, bacon, and toast. As he ate, he thought about Rob's Lizzie and the hell she must be enduring with those terrorists. With Emma safe, he could now focus all of his attention on the job at hand: rescuing Lizzie.

Michael watched as Rob pushed food around his plate. "You're going to need your strength." Michael gestured to Rob's uneaten breakfast.

"I can't think about anything other than Lizzie." Rob dejectedly moved the eggs to the other side of his bacon and then sipped his coffee.

"Promise me you will keep your strength up for this mission. I can't focus on retrieving Lizzie if I am worried about your ass getting shot," Michael said, placing a slice of bacon into his mouth. Rob didn't respond.

Just then, Rob's cell phone starting ringing. Rob looked at the number. "It's them. Hello?" he said, trying to hide his maddening rage.

"Hello, Rob. It looks like you are not playing for my side anymore," the terrorist sneered into his ear.

"What do you mean?" Rob asked meeting Michael's worried eyes. "I can still deliver the woman."

"Aren't you curious how I know you have help?" the terrorist asked calmly, which only served to increase Rob's frustration. He ran a hand over his unshaved face.

"It was me that arranged to take Emma and her notes from the DOD building yesterday."

Rob looked alarmed and wondered how they knew they were even at the DOD. *Someone must be following them. Did the terrorists know they had Ahmed?*

The hair on the back of Michael's neck stood on end. He didn't know what was being said, but whatever it was caused the blood to leave Rob's face.

"Tell me what you want. I have Emma, and I will deliver her to you tomorrow morning as originally agreed upon," Rob gushed into the receiver, trying to pacify the terrorist.

"I do believe you do not take my threats seriously," the terrorist said. "I am afraid I will have to kill the American woman to make my point."

"Do that and you can kiss Emma goodbye," Rob spat. "I know that prototype you obtained does not deliver the chemical agent. Emma was still working on the flaw in the design. She was still three weeks away from a working delivery system. I can bring her to you. You can do whatever you want to her to get your precious information, just as long as you keep the American woman alive."

Michael's eyes shot to Rob's. If he didn't trust his friend, he would have killed him for what he just said. Michael nodded his head up and down, encouraging Rob to continue. He knew there was no way Emma was stepping anywhere near the terrorist hold.

"Very well. Bring her. You have the advantage, as I do need her to make the system work. Once I have her, I will release the American woman. She is tough. I'll give her that. She hasn't once yet begged to die, and I know she is in a great deal of pain." The terrorist chuckled into the phone, raising Rob's blood pressure to dangerously high levels.

"I'll be there tomorrow at noon. Tell me where to drop the woman," Rob requested.

"I will text you the directions tomorrow at 1100 hours," the terrorist declared.

"Until then." Rob pressed the end button on the phone and looked down at his uneaten food. He could feel the bile rising in the back of his throat. He swallowed. Regaining his composure, Rob met the eyes of his brothers and explained the conversation.

"We have to leave now. I'm not waiting a second longer. Is everything packed and ready to go? If we drive straight through we can reach them at 0100 hours." Rob stood and scraped his uneaten food into the garbage can.

Just then all eyes turned to Emma coming into the kitchen. She was holding her side, but she was walking. A definite sight for Michael's sore eyes.

"Are you leaving now?" she asked, looking at Michael for confirmation of what she had just overheard Rob say. Michael met her eyes and nodded his head.

"I'll help you guys pack. But, Michael, before you leave, I just need a few minutes of your time." She walked to the table and started picking up plates and taking them into the kitchen.

"Tony. You're going to have to watch and make sure she doesn't overdo it." Michael walked up to her and removed a plate from her hand mid-scrape.

"She won't," Tony assured Michael as he looked sternly into Emma's eyes.

Emma cowered under the intense glare. She knew Tony meant business.

"Guys, wait here. Give Emma and me a minute alone please," Michael requested, knowing how anxious everyone was, knowing they only had a few precious minutes.

Michael led Emma into the living room, his hand on the small of her back. Just being near her threw him off center. How could he function in a normal environment knowing how she affected him? He led Emma to the other side of the room, away from the men, and they both looked out the window. Across the street the wind was battering some tangled wires and cables.

Michael stood behind Emma, wrapping his arms around her waist, careful to avoid her injury.

"What is it?" he whispered.

She felt the familiar tingle down her spine at his breath in her ear. She pushed back, closer to his chest.

"Promise me something before you go . . ." she begged Michael.

"Anything," he whispered, inhaling her earthly scent.

"Promise me that . . ." Emma stared at her feet. How could she tell Michael everything she felt for him? There weren't words to explain what she was feeling, and she had an extensive vocabulary. She didn't even know how to put words to her feelings, because she never bothered to name them or recognize them before. Words written by Gustave Flaubert from his novel *Madame Bovary* came to her mind, ". . . human speech is like a cracked kettle on which we tap crude rhythms for bears to dance to, while we long to make music that will melt the stars." The quote precisely summed up her feelings for Michael. She had no way to express them.

"What is it? You're starting to worry me," he whispered against her neck.

Gathering her courage and her assertiveness, she asked, "Promise that you will come back to me."

Michael exhaled the breath he didn't realize he was holding. "Emma, that is one promise I will gladly make."

"But you have to keep it, Michael," she said, fighting back the teardrops. If she looked at him now, she would lose it. He turned her around and met her glistening eyes. She saw the emotions reflected back to her. Tears streamed down her cheek, and he thumbed them away.

He lowered his mouth over hers in a possessive, mind-bending kiss. He communicated his promise to her through that kiss. She kissed him back with equal desperation. He walked over to his bag and removed a gun. He closed the distance in three strides and placed the gun in her upturned hand. "Take this. In case."

Her fingers closed around the gun. She felt safer having it. "Now you have to promise me something," he said, meeting her eyes. "Promise me you will be here waiting for me when I get back."

"I couldn't leave you now, Michael." She hoped she wasn't revealing too much with her statement.

He appreciated her sincere words. With promises spoken, he could continue with his mission. He leaned into her soft body one more time, pulling her closer to him. He kissed her again for good measure. Then he turned and left her standing alone in the living room.

CHAPTER NINETEEN

Michael, Rob, Steve, and Ahmed were barreling 75 miles per hour down the highway an hour outside of Pittsburgh. It had been a tension-packed, thirteen-hour drive straight through from Maine. Ahmed tried, unsuccessfully, to gain their sympathies.

"But I have a wife and two boys," Ahmed cried in the backseat. He knew he was going to die, along with the rest of the terrorists if these men were successful. And by the looks on their faces, they were going to be successful. His only hope was to escape once he showed them the house.

Michael knew he needed to contact Kevin, his brother who worked with Homeland Security. It was midnight, and he probably should have called earlier, but with everything else going on, it was now or never. He dug his cell phone out of his pocket and scrolled through his list until he came to Kevin's number. Kevin picked up on the third ring.

"Hello," he said in a sleep-filled voice.

"Kevin, it's Michael."

"What's going on? Do you know what time it is?" Kevin countered through the phone.

"Yeah, man, I know, and I'm sorry, but this couldn't wait."

Sensing the urgency in his brother's voice, Kevin became immediately alert. He walked into another room to avoid waking his wife.

"You're not going to be happy, man, but we need your help," Michael said.

"Who's we?" Kevin asked.

"Listen, it's a long story, but Rob, Steve, Tony and I need you on board with this. They have Lizzie," Michael beseeched, looking at Rob who was driving the car.

"Who does?" Kevin asked, confused.

Michael explained the condensed version of the situation to Rob, including the attempted kidnapping of Emma, until Kevin was pissed off that they hadn't contacted him sooner.

"What do you need me to do? You know I'll do it." Kevin exhaled. He had been holding his breath through the entire story. He couldn't believe his brothers, the men whom he served five tours with, left him out of this. Of course, he knew why. They had to do things he couldn't do given his current state of employment. But he was still pissed they wouldn't trust him enough to include him. He rationalized that that was exactly what they were doing now, including him, bringing him in when they didn't have a choice.

"We need this to be above reproach. None of us have clearance or authority anymore. But that isn't going to stop us. We're going to get Lizzie," Michael stated.

"Where is this going down?" Kevin asked, praying to God it was somewhere within driving distance.

"Homestead. Your backyard," Michael said, thankful Kevin worked for the Homeland Security building in Pittsburgh.

"Thank God! Otherwise, coordination would take days," Kevin said, pulling his pants on with one hand. He slipped into a t-shirt and sat down to tie up his boots. "I can have a five-man team ready in under two hours," Kevin said,

"Thank you, Kevin. We have to be in on this though. We found Ahmed. We're taking Lizzie out of there. And we certainly are having a hand in taking down those motherfuckers," Michael declared.

"Of course. I'll talk to my boss. He'll be relieved that this closure will come in under our office. But we need to take as many alive as we can," Kevin said, scribbling a note to his wife. He grabbed his keys from the tray on the table nearest his door and locked his six deadbolts from the outside.

"Rendezvous at this address." Kevin rattled it off as Michael programmed it into the GPS.

"How long will it take you to get there?" Kevin asked, sliding into the front seat of his car.

"It says about twenty minutes," Michael said. "But, Kevin, we don't want any shit on this. We are going in. If you can't guarantee your boss will be on board, we're going straight to the hold up. I must be clear, you must be clear, we're the ones bringing Lizzie out," Michael challenged.

"Michael, I know you don't trust a governmental agency not to keep you tied up with red tape, but trust me. I'll make it so that you, Rob, and Steve are in on the takedown. Rob will be the one to bring Lizzie out," Kevin reassured his friend as he sped down the highway towards his office.

"Thank you, Kevin. I knew we could count on you. We'll see you soon." Michael pressed the end button and relayed the conversation to his brothers.

They pulled into an empty parking lot fifteen minutes later. Rob pulled into the spot closest to the door. About five minutes later, Kevin pulled in next to Rob. They all got out of their cars and Kevin greeted each one of his brothers. God, it was good to see them. He made sure to make eye contact and hug each one of the men who had saved his life on more than one occasion. He gave an evil eye to Ahmed. Having a terrorist, alive, in his office, would get him anything he needed. He would make sure this went down the right way, with their assistance. He gave his guarantee to his brothers that they would be held harmless for their actions, which would fall under the guise of Homeland Security. It was a small price to pay for these men he was bound to for the rest of his life. He knew, without doubt, that they would be there for him.

Rob pushed Ahmed in front of the men who followed Kevin to the outer door. Kevin pulled out his security card and swiped the card reader to gain entrance into the building. Then Kevin had to briefly explain his visitors to the officers stationed at the security desk. They were granted entrance to the elevators where Kevin swiped his access card, and pressed the button for the third floor.

Once inside the bullpen, he telephoned his boss and the five-man team. They were all set to arrive in the next twenty minutes. It was now 0045 hours. It wouldn't be long before Rob got to hold Lizzie again. Michael wondered how Emma was doing with Tony. He knew he didn't have to worry about the terrorists, but that still left Special Agent Daniel Ingrams. If he didn't trust Kevin, he would not have made contact with a federal agency at all. Other than Kevin, Michael had no idea whom he could trust.

"Promise me something," Michael continued to the men at his side. "Promise me that we won't risk Emma again."

The men nodded.

The team arrived at the same time as their boss. The men got to their feet as they entered the bullpen. If Kevin wasn't able to convince his boss, then Michael guessed they would be spending the next few years in prison, and he could kiss the future he hoped to create with Emma goodbye.

"In my office, Kevin. And bring the prisoner," his boss commanded.

Kevin led Ahmed to the office on the upper floor of the bullpen. His boss had Kevin close the door. Kevin explained the situation to his boss and his relationship to the men who stood in the bullpen. He explained how they needed to be a part of this takedown and were highly trained Green Berets six months out of the military. After Kevin's explanation and information gathered from Ahmed, his boss acquiesced.

"Just so we are clear, you three will follow my orders. This is a hostage retrieval mission, and I will permit you there, armed, but my team takes lead," the boss asserted, looking the men square in the eyes. If any of them had a problem, he needed to know now. Rob, Steve, and Michael agreed.

"Let's get Lizzie," Rob announced to the men as they geared up for war.

CHAPTER
TWENTY

The men traveled to the city of Homestead and found the quiet neighborhood of Munhall. The porch lights shown from the road as they traveled past the well-maintained 1920s era homes. It was there that the terrorists were holed up in a two-story, brick house.

After further interrogation of Ahmed, the men learned there were three men left in the cell. It originally started with five, but the guard Michael killed, and Ahmed in their custody, left three in the house. Three terrorists in the house plus Lizzie.

Pulling up the layout of the home on a real estate website, they learned the house had four bedrooms and a full basement. They assumed the bedrooms were located on the second floor of the house as was standard of the construction in that area.

As they drove by the home at 0130 hours, they noticed how well the terrorists' house blended in with the other two-story colonials. If asked later on media reports, the neighbors would say they had no idea what was occurring in the house as the men kept to themselves. They would also say they only noticed two men ever coming or going from the home.

Rob bounced his leg up and down, causing the van to shake. He was anxious to get to his Lizzie. "I just have to get her out, Michael." Rob stared into Michael's eyes. Being so close, yet so far away was torture. A million things could go wrong. "I am scared to death I am going to find her tied to a bed, already dead," Rob confessed.

"You can't think that way. You have to keep hope alive, Rob." Michael looked at his brother's ragged face. Rob hadn't shaved in at least a month. This wasn't the first time Michael had seen Rob with facial hair. It was common for the Unit, while on tour in Afghanistan, to grow beards. Typically, the Army frowned on facial hair, but they needed to blend in with the locals. They even held a contest. Who could grow the nicest beard? Rob always won.

As Michael looked at his best friend now, he didn't sense any of the previous comradery or the levity that took over after being in an incredibly tense situation for months on end. A situation where one could die in an instant. While they were serious in combat, there was something about bombs dropping twenty feet from where you slept that allowed the men to find the humor in life. What were they going to do, cry about it? That wouldn't have served their mission well.

As they pulled into a parking spot on the street a block down from the terrorist hold up, Rob turned to his friend. "I'm scared. I wasn't scared in Afghanistan, but I'm scared now."

Empathizing with his friend, Michael knew the fear that Rob felt. He felt it too both times Emma was taken from him. "We're gonna get her back, man. I know it's hard, but you have to keep the faith," Michael said, touching Rob's shoulder.

"Pray with me," Rob pleaded, his eyes meeting Michael's. Michael acquiesced, and they bowed their heads.

"God, I know we haven't spoken in about seven months, but I am coming to you now. Please let my Lizzie be alive. Everything else we can handle, but she has to be alive. I don't know what I would do without her, God. Please, God. You know I have always been a good Christian. I have served my country well. The only thing I have ever asked is that you keep Lizzie safe. Please don't let me down now, God. Please let me find her alive. It is in your name that I pray and I thank you, Amen." Michael squeezed Rob's hand in the stillness of the van's backseat.

Michael met Rob's frightened eyes and saw tears. For those few moments, all the danger of the night, all of the thoughts of terrorists, and foiling a plot fled in the sacred quietness of the backseat of the van. Michael sat with Rob and held his hand. He knew Rob needed the reassurance and the comfort that only another person, one who fully understood the gravity of the situation, could offer.

Rob was quick to wipe away his tears, but he knew there was a very real possibility that Lizzie was already dead. Michael knew Rob may not survive if Lizzie wasn't found alive.

The men, sensing Rob and Michael needed a moment, waited quietly on the street. They had opened the back of the vans, grabbing their gear bags and removing their weaponry. Rob looked at Michael one last time, silently pleading with his brother to do all he could. Michael wouldn't let his best friend down. After all they experienced in war, the endless nights of shelling, the raids on Al-Qaida hold ups in the middle of the night, the constant danger of life in a war zone, they would make it through this, too. Rob had never once faltered in his unwavering support of Michael and his fears. He wouldn't let Rob down now. He would take out the three terrorists himself if he had to . . . to get to Lizzie. They weren't sure where Lizzie was being held. All Ahmed could say was she was in one of the four bedrooms, and the last he had seen her, she was tied to the bed with heavy ropes.

"What kind of rope was she tied with," Rob spat into Ahmed's face.

"It was a double-braid, nylon rope. Her skin was rubbed raw from trying to escape. If she would have just accepted her fate, then she wouldn't have so many rope burns," Ahmed said as convincingly as possible.

Rob grabbed Ahmed by his windbreaker and gathered it at the neck, effectually cutting off his air supply.

"We still need him, man," Michael countered as he placed his hands over Rob's. Michael pried Rob's hands away from Ahmed's neck.

"Tell me exactly how you left her?" Rob demanded of Ahmed. Ahmed had been with the men for the last two days.

"When I left her, her hands and feet were bound to the frame of the bed. Her legs were spread to allow the men easy access."

Rob knew they had raped her, but he had no idea how often. These weren't men they were dealing with. These were savages. They didn't deserve the quick death they would receive tonight. They deserved to be tortured even worse than the way they had tortured Ahmed. If it was up to him, each man would be strung up by his balls, and he would cut off their dicks. Then he would shove their dicks into their mouths and leave them to bleed out. Rob wanted revenge and justice for what Lizzie had endured.

"Did they give her water and food?" Rob demanded as his face contorted, afraid of the answer.

"Just water I think. They weren't feeding her. They would have to hand feed her, and they didn't expect her to make it this long," Ahmed said, meeting Rob's ravaged green eyes.

Again Rob charged Ahmed. This time Michael's hands made it to Rob's chest, keeping him a foot from where Ahmed stood, his wrists bound with zip ties. Rob had the look of death in his stinging, lifeless eyes. Michael knew Rob would kill Ahmed given the chance.

"Let's focus on getting her out," Michael ordered, pushing against Rob's chest.

Rob sagged at Michael's words. He knew Michael was right. They walked to the back of the van. The Homeland Security team was ready to go. M4 rifles hung over their shoulders, and Sig Sauer P226's in their side holsters were attached to their thighs. Michael and Rob suited up. They wore bulletproof vests, armed themselves with the same rifles and pistols of the five-man team, and put their bulletproof helmets on. They secured Ahmed in the back of the van with handcuffs.

"I don't have to tell you what's at risk." Michael faced the other men. "Lizzie is in the house, presumed alive. They have the field notes and prototype of a Top Secret government project with them. It is our job to retrieve Lizzie and the information on the prototype. Emma's work cannot make it into the hands of terrorists. If that happens, the U. S. is in grave danger." He looked at the men to whom he was about to trust with his life, as well as Lizzie's. Thank God Emma was safely at Rob's house with Tony watching after her.

"Secure Lizzie. Then find the information on the prototype. I understand you want these terrorists taken alive, and I promise to do my best to make that happen. But make no mistake, Lizzie is the number one priority," Michael said, looking straight into Rob's eyes.

Rob appreciated the pep talk and had a new look of determination on his face. He was about to get his Lizzie back.

At 0200 hours, they were ready to breach the house.

CLOSER

The men walked in standard formation, hugging the shadows of the night. They had the element of surprise on their side. The terrorists were falsely secure in their knowledge, thinking Rob was delivering Emma tomorrow. They had no idea Ahmed was with them or that their adversaries had killed the guard. The brothers only had to take down three men. They had conducted this same mission numerous times over their five tours together. The only thing different about this mission— the most important difference—was that emotions were involved. Michael needed Rob to push his emotions to the side and accomplish the mission. He hadn't lost faith in his friend. He believed he could do it.

The eight-man team approached the side entrance. One of the men from Homeland Security took point and breached the door. The terrorists had booby trapped it with a bomb. A homemade claymore mine was rigged to explode upon entrance. However, due to the age of the house, the door wasn't sealed properly from the rain and snow. The claymore had become saturated, and upon breach, only one-quarter of the homemade device exploded.

The leading man fell to the ground. Wooden door pieces and metal shrapnel littered his guts. He wouldn't make it out alive. They didn't have time to devote to the man lying on the ground. The sound surely alerted the terrorists to their presence. They busted through the remnants of the door and found themselves in a cheaply furnished den filled with overflowing ashtrays.

Quickly clearing the basement, they took the stairs quietly two at a time. They opened the door at the top of the stairs and found themselves in a hallway to the left of the kitchen. They quickly cleared the downstairs and made their way up to the second floor.

Just then a terrorist fired his rifle, backing down the hallway and trying to make it into one of the bedrooms. Michael's accurate shot left the terrorist dead on the ground. Another terrorist fired at the team. The seven men easily outnumbered the man armed with an AK-47 Soviet rifle, who ducked behind a wall. With one shot from their team, they entered the room to find the terrorist lying on the carpet, blood pooling around his chest. This was probably the bastard who raped Lizzie, Michael thought. He looked the man dead in the eye and pulled the trigger of his rifle, putting a bullet through his skull. How he would love the terrorists to suffer after everything they did to Lizzie and to Emma.

The men had cleared three of the four bedrooms, which meant the bedroom at the end of the hallway contained Lizzie and the remaining terrorist.

A hostage negotiator on the DHS team spoke in Algerian through the bedroom door. Although Michael recognized a few words, he couldn't follow the conversation. They waited for hours. They couldn't risk breaching the door and the terrorist killing Lizzie. They had to let the negotiator do his thing. After numerous back and forth conversations, often one-sided, the terrorist was instructed to open the door and place his hands on the top of his head. The terrorist opened the door and backed up into the room. He placed his hands on the top of his head and was apprehended in a matter of seconds. Homeland Security had one terrorist plus Ahmed. That would have to be enough.

Rob pushed past the men and made his way into the bedroom. He found Lizzie lying unconscious on the bed. He fell to his knees as a cry escaped his throat. His anguish could be heard four houses down. Rob heaved and sobbed as Michael went to his side. Rob gathered his strength and gently untied his Lizzie from her position. He took notice of the blood that had gathered on the mattress between her thighs where the men had savagely raped her.

"Y . . . You . . . have to do it . . . man. You have to tell me . . . Mich . . . Michael. I can't. I can't do it," he said in a rush that left him deflated, sitting with his shoulder propped up against the bed. He gently cradled Lizzie's hand in his, softly stroking her skin. He kissed her hand and his tear-filled eyes pleaded with Michael's.

Michael did not want to be the one to tell his best friend what the rest of the men already knew. Michael placed his forefinger and middle finger against her carotid artery and felt for a pulse. Nothing. Michael's eyes glistened as he looked at his broken friend. Michael slowly shook his head, so he offered no false hope to Rob. Rob cried so hard, no sound escaped his mouth. He didn't inhale for minutes on end as he exhaled his anguish. After what felt like an eternity, Rob turned desperate. He scrambled up to Lizzie's side, gathering her cold body into his arms. He heaved and sobbed over his Lizzie. Michael stood next to the bed feeling almost as helpless as he did when Ingrams had taken Emma.

How will Rob ever come back from this, Michael wondered as he watched his friend rock his lifeless fiancée back and forth in his arms.

"Let's give him some time," Michael said to the men in the room.

One by one, the men patted Rob's shoulder in a sign of solidarity as they exited the room. They still had to find the field notes and prototype, plus any other booby trap the terrorists had left. One of the men ran back to check on the injured man who was put down by the initial breach of the door. He was still alive but wouldn't be for much longer if they didn't get him some help. The man radioed for an ambulance, rattling off the address. Michael knew what it felt like to lose a member of one's team. It brought back feelings of Leroy, who he had failed to save on that fateful August afternoon.

After an hour of fruitless searching of the house, the men needed to search the room that contained a distraught Rob and a deceased Lizzie. Michael made his way back to the bedroom at the end of the hallway. He found Rob in the same position, although his demeanor had changed. Rob now sat lifeless still holding Lizzie. He was stroking her hair away from her face in an effort to calm himself. One look at Rob, and Michael knew he was in shock: his lips were a faint blue, his breathing was rapid and shallow. Michael touched his friend's arm, and his skin felt cool and clammy. Rob needed medical attention, but Michael didn't, for the life of him, understand how he was going to separate Lizzie from his embrace. Just then, the coroner arrived with a stretcher. He met Michael's eyes and read the warning in them. The corner stood off to the side of the room, ready.

"Rob. You have to let her go." Michael looked at his helpless friend. "She's gone, man, and you need to be treated."

"What the fuck am I supposed to do now?" Rob whispered as he folded into himself.

"You get up and you let Lizzie go. I know you don't want to hear this, but you must have been preparing for this possibility," Michael gently said as he placed his hand on Rob's shoulder.

"Fuck you, man!" Rob spat out at Michael. "She was all I had. No one else but her. How the fuck am I supposed to live without her?"

"We can talk about that later. Your lips are blue, man. We need to get you treated," Michael persuaded as he squeezed Rob's shoulder.

Rob looked down on his Lizzie with love-filled eyes. He gently released her and laid her back down on the bed. He pressed his lips to her cold forehead and lingered there.

"Rob?" Michael said in a calming voice.

"Just give me a fucking minute, please," Rob begged, staring at his Lizzie.

Michael backed away and did as his friend had bid. Michael would forever be worried about his best friend. He was truly without knowledge about how to help him cope.

Rob pressed another kiss to his Lizzie, this time saying goodbye. He stood and met Michael's eyes. Michael saw how absolutely destroyed his friend was. Michael guided Rob down the stairs to the waiting ambulance.

"I don't need to go. I'm fine," Rob croaked as the EMT took his blood pressure.

It had dropped to dangerously low levels. Michael had always heard about dying of a broken heart, but he never thought it possible, that was until this exact moment.

"Just go with them. When I finish here, I promise I'll come and get you. Then we can figure out what needs to be done," Michael appealed to his best friend.

Totally defeated, Rob allowed the woman to put him on a stretcher and place an oxygen mask over his face. Confident Rob's physical body would be taken care of, Michael headed back into the house. He still hadn't found the field notes or prototype.

He walked back into the room where Lizzie had died and looked at the death bed. Michael stood silently weeping for his friend for a few minutes as he stared at the bed. His thoughts turned to Emma. What if it had been Emma in Lizzie's place? He hadn't known Emma as long as Rob had known Lizzie, yet he still felt her in his very soul. Losing her would be like losing himself. Is that how Rob felt, like he no longer knew who he was outside of him and Lizzie? Had he wrapped up his world in Lizzie so much he now had to carve a new world for himself? Michael knew that was how he felt about Emma. He worshipped her. The two times he failed to protect her would forever haunt him. Not saving Leroy didn't feel close to how he felt about allowing Emma to get hurt, and Leroy was one of his best friends.

Michael could only imagine Rob's pain, but at the same time, he didn't want to. He didn't want to put Emma in that position, even in his mind. He took out his phone and dialed Tony.

"Hello?" Tony said on the second ring.

Michael remained silent, unsure of what to say as fear gripped his soul, so he stood breathing into the phone.

"Michael? What happened? Did you find Lizzie?"

Finally Michael remembered his reason for calling. "How's Emma? Is she safe?" Michael pleaded.

"She's fine. She was upstairs asleep the last time I checked on her. I gave her another shot for the pain.

"Check on her for me. Make sure she is all right. Please. I need to know before I can move from this spot." Michael didn't care what he was revealing to one of his best friends. He had to know.

"Hold on, I'll run upstairs and check," Tony said as he made his ways upstairs and into the guest bedroom. He watched Emma's chest softly rise and fall. "She's fine. Sleeping peacefully," Tony answered his distraught friend.

"Lizzie's dead. We didn't make it in time," Michael said, feeling his gut clench with guilt as he said the dreadful words.

"Oh. My. God. How is Rob?" Tony was quick to ask.

"He's in bad shape. I honestly don't know how he is going to make it back from this," Michael said. "I convinced him to let her go after an hour, and then finally managed to get him in the back of an ambulance. The last time I saw him, he was being carted away to the hospital."

"What can I do?" Tony asked helplessly.

"Please watch over Emma. Do not let anyone near her. Promise me you will kill whoever tries to come into that house who isn't me or Steve," Michael begged his comrade.

"I'll watch over her like she is mine. I promise. Nothing will happen to Emma as long as I'm alive," Tony reassured a genuinely tormented Michael.

"Thank you, Tony," Michael croaked on his own tears. He didn't even care if Tony could hear him crying. He was so relieved that she was fine, yet he felt such guilt that Rob and Lizzie weren't.

Michael ended the call, shaking all feelings from his mind. He had a mission to complete. He began ransacking the bedroom that had been the torture chamber for Lizzie. He knew the crime scene folks from Homeland Security wanted in, but he had to find the information before that could happen. He searched high and low and failed to find anything. Then he thought to flip up the blood and fluid stained mattress Lizzie had been lying on. When he did, he found Emma's notebooks and the Hummingbird. Confident in recovering the missing items, he turned the room over to the forensics' team. He took his findings back to the remaining members of the team.

Kevin was at the van waiting with Ahmed.
Kevin had moved the van to the front of the house
where the terrorists were holed up so he could
coordinate liaisons with his office and his boss.
Michael approached with the information in hand. He
had to tell Kevin everything about Emma's project,
even though Emma wouldn't be happy with that
disclosure. They had needed Kevin's help, and he had
come through in a big way. He knew that one of his
best friends wouldn't let him down, and he knew that
he would get the same unwavering support now.

"Do you have everything?" Kevin asked Michael.

"Yep. This is everything. We need to get it back
to Emma and the DOD before someone realizes it is
missing," Michael said, meeting Kevin's fixed eyes.

"Michael. You aren't going to be happy, but I had
to inform my boss of everything to get the help you
needed."

"I understand, and I appreciate the risk you took
in helping us," Michael reassured his friend.

"That's not the worst of it, Michael," Kevin
cautioned, meeting Michael eye for eye.

"What? What could be worse than what we found tonight?" Michael asked dejectedly.

"My boss had to call the DOD and let them know exactly what was happening,"

"How the fuck could you let that happen? Emma could lose her job for what she did," Michael raged, his emotions finally taking hold of him. Tonight, Michael had experienced a wide range of different emotions. Seeing his best friend ruined undid him. He couldn't contain his feelings when it came to the guilt he felt about the fact that Emma was alive but Rob had lost his Lizzie.

Michael quickly turned from Kevin. He did not want Kevin to see him lose his composure.

Kevin waited for Michael to gather himself. He knew what losing Lizzie did to him. He could only imagine what it did to Michael. Kevin had no problem empathizing with Rob. He had a wife at home whom he adored.

Michael turned back around, determination in his eyes. "She can't lose her job. It means everything to her."

"I will do everything in my power to see to it that that doesn't happen," Kevin promised.

"I know you will, Kevin. I appreciate everything you've done already. I don't mean to take it out on you or to sound ungrateful. You kept us clean tonight and out of jail. For that, I owe you. If you can keep Emma from losing her job, well, I guess I will owe you even more," Michael apologized. "So? What do we do now?"

"Why don't we check in on Rob? See how he is doing. The next few months, hell, *years*, are going to be the worst of Rob's life," Kevin said.

"Yeah. We will. What about the information?" Michael asked.

"Give it to me, and I'll make sure it gets back to the DOD." Kevin motioned for Michael to hand everything over.

Kevin took Ahmed, Michael, and Steve back to his office. They spent the next four hours in debriefing. Michael confessed everything, even his hand in the attempted kidnapping of Emma, and his reasons for doing it. Michael told Homeland he didn't want the hundred grand the terrorist deposited in his bank account.

"Good, because we have to confiscate that money anyway," Kevin's boss told Michael.

"No problem," Michael said as he wrote down his account number for the man.

Homeland Security was confident Michael was innocent of any wrongdoing and let Steve and him go after an exhausting interview. By the time Steve, Michael, and Kevin left the office, the sun was coming up. They had to check on Rob.

They walked to Kevin's SUV, and Kevin drove the men in silence to UPMS Presbyterian Hospital. They asked for directions to Rob's room from the candy striper at the information desk.

They followed her instructions and stood outside of a closed door to room 932.

"Excuse me, nurse?" Michael asked the nurse passing by in the hallway.

"Yes. How can I help you?"

"Why is this door closed? We'd like to visit our friend."

"I'm sorry. The doctor is in with him now. As soon as the door opens, you may go in," she advised them.

The three men remained silent as they leaned up against the wall outside of Rob's room. No one knew exactly what to say at the gravity of such a loss.

"How can we even comfort him?" Steve asked, breaking the silence.

"We stay supportive and listen. We stay positive. We help him through this. We help with the funeral arrangements. When is Lizzie's body being released?" Michael turned looking to Kevin.

"The coroner won't be done with the autopsy for another day or two, so that gives you some time to make the arrangements," Kevin responded, reflecting Michael's anxious stare. Michael stood leaning against the wall, chewing on his bottom lip, thinking about his devastated friend. Suddenly the door opened and the doctor exited.

Michael, Steve, and Kevin made their way inside the room. Rob had been given a private room, no doubt because of his emotional state. What they saw in the bed shocked them, and that was saying something because these men had seen the other side of hell. Rob smiled as the men walked into the room.

"What's with the long faces?" Rob asked, clearly in denial of the night before.

"How are you holding up?" Michael asked.

"They're letting me go. I finally can get home to Lizzie," Rob said, his eyes smiling.

How was Michael going to break the news to Rob a second time? The first time nearly killed him.

"What do you remember about last night, Rob?" Michael asked.

"I remember we rescued Lizzie, and I'm stuck here away from her. Why hasn't she come to see me?" Rob questioned his friends.

It was Michael's job, as Rob's closest brother, to break the bad news for a second time in as so many hours. "Rob, we found Lizzie last night, but we were too late. She died before we could reach her." Michael looked to Rob to gauge his emotional reaction. Rob's smile immediately turned downward. His eyes filled with tears.

"What do you mean? I held her in my arms. I kissed her head. I stoked her hair," Rob whispered.

Michael looked into Rob's mournful eyes. "Yes you did. But, Rob, she was already gone. You were saying goodbye."

"Get the fuck out! How can you say such a thing about Lizzie? Get the fuck out, now." Rob met Michael's eyes with fierce determination.

"We are not leaving you. Not right now. Not until we know you won't do anything stupid." Michael continued, "We love you, man. We know you're hurting. Let us be here for you, the way you are always there for us. You lost your Lizzie, man. We need to be here for you because we lost her, too. She belonged to all of us to protect. We are brothers. I would never, ever lie to you about something like this."

Tears fell silently down Rob's face. He needed his mother. His mother could make it all right. "Call my mother. Tell her what happened. Tell her I need her. Please," Rob beseeched Michael.

Michael got out his phone and asked for her number.

A few minutes later, Michael turned back to Rob and said, "She's on her way. She'll meet you at your house. When are they letting you go?"

"They're gathering the discharge papers now. There is nothing physically wrong with me." He laughed a sadistic laugh.

Michael looked at a discarded needle in the trash bin, thinking the doctors must have prescribed a sedative. Down the hall they could hear a child crying. He found himself folding a blanket that was falling off Rob's bed, as if straightening the room would keep Rob safe.

Michael exchanged looks with his brothers. They were going to have to remain constantly at his side for the next couple of days, or they would be planning another funeral.

CHAPTER
TWENTY-THREE

The men made the long thirteen-hour drive back to Rob's house. Michael was excited with nervous energy at the thought of being with Emma again. But then again he felt incredibly guilty as his friend rode solemnly in the backseat of the car. They hadn't talked much on the ride home. There was nothing more to be said that could help Rob with the tragedy of losing Lizzie. Every once in a while, Rob would break down, and they would watch in amazement at how he would pull himself back together again. Over the course of the drive home, it became a vicious cycle. With each breakdown came tears, punching the car seat in front of him, and curse words directed at his fellow passengers. Michael wondered how long it would be before Rob started blaming Emma and him for Lizzie's death. They were, after all, the delay in retrieving Lizzie. Were they the reason that ultimately cost her life?

Michael still had the ability to think rationally. It wasn't Emma or him that cost Lizzie her life. It was the terrorists. No one could be blamed but the bastards that kidnapped her, raped her, and eventually killed her. Surely Rob would come to see that, although

Michael expected he wouldn't be thinking rationally anytime soon.

Rob grew angrier and angrier as they drove to his house. His tirades about the failure of his friends were becoming stronger. And then he asked it. He asked the question that everyone was waiting for him to ask.

"Why didn't we get to her sooner?" Rob cried, looking at Michael.

Michael had never lied to his best friend, and he wouldn't start now. "Remember, Rob, we had to drive back to Maine to get the information the terrorists requested and then Emma got kidnapped."

"Oh right, saving Emma took precedence over saving Lizzie," Rob spat back.

"Rob," Michael cautioned, "try to remember exactly what occurred. The same terrorists kidnapped Emma, and we were right there."

"Yeah, but you've only known Emma for less than a week. What made her more important than getting Lizzie?" Rob asked, his voice rising in volume.

"We were right there. We couldn't just let Emma be taken, too. We had to do something. I am sorry if you feel like that is in some way responsible for Lizzie's death," Michael said, his guilt eating him alive.

"Stop the car!" Rob ordered as he started to open the door. Steve managed to pull off the side of the highway and slam on the brakes at the same time before Rob had his door completely opened. Once outside, Rob paced back and forth like a caged animal. Michael knew Rob needed to release his feelings of rage, and he was a good enough friend to stick around for his accusations when he knew Rob needed him.

Michael started to open his car door, but Steve placed a hand on his arm. "You are both my brothers, but I won't let him kill you," Steve reassured Michael before he exited the car.

"You forget who you're talking to. I won't let him kill me either," Michael said, mentally preparing himself for the fight that was about to ensue.

"You forget. He has nothing to lose," Steve cautioned Michael.

"You're right. Don't let him kill me," Michael said. Thinking better of the situation, Michael exited the car.

Rob ambushed Michael in four long strides. He was in his face before Michael could even catch his breath. *This was going to hurt.*

Rob screamed, muted by the cars passing by at high speeds on the highway, "This is your fault! The reason Lizzie is dead is all your fault!" Rob spat onto Michael's face. Michael could feel Rob's warm breath on his check. "If we weren't so fucking worried about Emma, if you were more concentrated on Lizzie, she would still be alive." Rob hauled his arm back and jabbed Michael in the stomach.

Michael bent over at the loss of breath. Rob connected again. This time with an uppercut to Michael's jaw. Michael staggered backwards. He would allow his brother a couple more before he started fighting back. Rob stalked forward, his left leg slightly behind his right. Rob connected with Michael's chest in a chamber punch.

Michael knew he had to start fighting back soon or Rob would render him immobilized. Michael steadied himself in a combat stance, left leg behind his right one. He angled his body and went onto his tip toes. He was ready and waiting for Rob to approach again. Michael rationalized that, after a good fight, Rob would have it out of his system and could move on to grieving. Little did Michael know that anger was the second stage in the grief process. Rob was grieving over losing his Lizzie—his life.

With Michael at the ready, Rob approached. Rob dodged to the left. Michael swung to the left, doing a 360-degree back turn, adding extra momentum to the swing, and connected with Rob's face. Rob staggered back several steps. Apparently, Rob was only going to allow Michael one punch because he charged for Michael's legs. Michael fell backwards and landed hard on the asphalt, hitting the back of his head on the way down. Rob had Michael pinned and was driving his fist into Michael's face. Michael bucked his hips, trying to rid himself of Rob, but Rob remained steady. Rob bloodied his face and ears until all his fight was gone.

Steve had decided to intervene about the same time Rob stopped pummeling Michael. Steve helped an exhausted and deflated Rob to his feet. Then he went to Michael's feet and reached out his hand. It turned out Rob had beat the crap out of Michael, and he required Steve to lift him from under his armpits to stand. Once upright, Michael started to stagger disoriented into traffic. Steve caught him and directed him to the backseat of the car. He had left Rob sitting on the hood.

Once Michael was secure and passed out in the back, Steve walked to the front of the vehicle. Rob reached out, pulling Steve into an intimate embrace. They were brothers, and they hugged like brothers for as long as Rob needed. Rob was the one to break away, wiping tears from his eyes. He had just beaten the shit out of his best friend, and he knew, beyond a doubt, that the tough son-of-a-bitch let him. Rob was truly humbled.

They returned to the car and continued their drive in silence. They reached Rob's house without further incident, only stopping to use the bathroom. Steve checked on Michael occasionally, making sure he was still breathing. He probably needed a hospital, but Rob promised to fix him up when they reached the house. Michael was passed out until about thirty minutes outside of Lewiston when he regained consciousness and tried desperately to sit up.

"Michael," Rob exhaled, clearly worried about his best friend. "Look. I know what you did back there for me, and I appreciate it. More than you will ever know," Rob said humbly to a battered, bloodied, and bruised face.

"Do you feel any better?" Michael coughed mid-sentence from the blood that coated his throat.

"No. Now I feel worse for what I did to you." Rob apologized, trying to make eye contact through the tiny slits that served as Michael's eyes.

"You didn't do anything to me I wasn't willing to let you do. You know me. If I wanted to stop it, I would have," Michael reassured his friend. "Do you remember why we decided to save Emma? This is important to me, man. You have to remember the logical reasons behind why we did what we did. You are my closest friend. I can't lose you, man," Michael implored through his swollen lips.

"I remember. I remember everything. I don't blame you or Emma," Rob professed.

Thank God, Michael thought. Emma didn't need Rob's anger directed at her during her recovery period. The thought of Emma was what gave Michael the strength to endure his beating.

"I know where the blame lies, and by my calculations, we killed three of the five of them," Rob said.

"Yes, we did, brother!" Michael attempted to smile through the pain. "And the other two will serve out the remainder of their days in prison cells. So, how are you really?" Michael asked.

"Truthfully, I don't know. It hasn't sunk in yet. I do feel awful about what I did to you."

"Ah!" said Michael. "Remember, I let you do it."

"If you say so," Rob bantered.

It was good that Rob started to return to himself. He had a long, painful road ahead, but this beating freed some of his more base emotions. Rob continued to silently sob the remainder of the ride home. These men had seen him scared, seen him brave, and now they had seen him broken. These men knew him inside and out. He trusted them with his soul, which is why he allowed himself to cry in front of them. *Or so he told himself.*

By the time they arrived, the sun was beginning to set. They got out of the car and staggered their way down the front walk as the sun dropped below the horizon.

CLOSER

Emma lay awake upstairs in her bed, thinking about the last time she was with Michael. She longed to feel his lips on her skin. She ached to feel him deep inside her. Would he come back to her? Once the terrorist threat was taken care of, would he still want her with the same ferocity that he wanted her with before?

After an hour of trying to get comfortable, she gave up and figured a hot shower was in order. She needed to clean out her flesh wound, and the hot water would wash away her stress. She spent a good, long twenty minutes in the shower, letting the warmth wash over her body. She took great care to wash the wound with soap. It still burned when anything touched it, but it felt a hundred times better than when she was shot two days ago. Her movements were still limited. She could walk around the house and had even cooked dinner for Tony that night.

With the hot water spraying her naked body, she once again thought of Michael. She prayed on more than two occasions that he come back to her in one piece. She knew how dangerous these terrorists could be, stopping at nothing to reach their desired end. One

had shot her. They were ruthless. And the torture
Michael had to put Ahmed through before he gave up
the information just proved how dedicated they were to
achieving that end. She prayed Michael was all right.
She prayed no one got hurt. She prayed Michael still
wanted her the same way she still wanted him. If
anything, after he'd gone on such a dangerous mission,
she wanted him all the more. Flesh wound be damned,
she would have him when he returned home to her.
Funny, this wasn't her home, yet she thought of it as
such because this is where Michael would be returning.

She turned off the water and stepped onto the
floor mat in the guest bathroom. She dried herself off
and slowly dressed in her shorts and a tank top—
standard issue sleeping attire when she was alone.
Sure, she owned a negligee or two but had yet to wear
one for Michael. She couldn't wait to get Michael back
to her house so she could try one on for him. How
would he react to seeing her dressed in scandalous see-
through lace and a thong? She hoped he would rip the
clothes from her body. She liked it when he was rough
with her. She remembered him ripping the panties from
her body the first night they were together and then
smelling them. His reaction had been so primal. There
was an extreme amount of power in knowing she did
that to him. She drove him to his base urges.

As she was dressing, she heard a car door slam
and then another. She finished putting on her top and
then raced to the front window. The sight took her
breath away. There were three men walking slowly
down the front walk towards the door. Michael was

following Steve and Rob, so she couldn't get a good look at Michael.

Where's Lizzie, she thought as she raced down the hallway to the stairs.

She reached the bottom step the same time the men entered the door. Her breath caught in her throat and tears immediately fell from her eyes. She looked at a battered Michael and ran to him, throwing her arms around his neck and pulling him to her body. Thoughts of Lizzie fled her mind as they were replaced with thoughts of Michael.

"What happened?" she asked, lightly touching Michael's swollen lips.

Michael winced, still sore from his beating. He shook his head, indicating he didn't want to talk about it.

"Not now. I'll tell you later," Michael said, making eye contact with Rob before Rob bowed his head.

She would have to wait for an explanation on Michael's condition. She didn't want to push, not right now. She looked to Rob.

"Where's Lizzie?" she innocently asked Rob.

Rob had just gained his composure. He didn't want to lose it again, not in front of Emma. "We were too late," Rob whispered, bowing his head, careful to avoid Emma's eyes. If he saw sympathy there, he would lose it all over again.

Emma let go of Michael and stepped away. She found the couch and sat down, waiting for an explanation. She looked up from her hands as Tony entered the room. He sat down next to her. "So, fill us in," Tony said to Rob and Steve.

Michael joined Emma on the couch and tucked her safely under his arm. He had missed her something fierce. He just needed to touch her, even just her shoulder to reassure himself that he had made all of the right decisions. He needed to breathe, and touching her allowed him to do that. Once she was safely in his arms, he met her gaze. His eyes misted up but not from the pain. Tears started to fall at the thought they had traded Emma's life for Lizzie's. Guilt was a bitch and he was feeling it right now. He pressed his forehead against hers and lingered there while Steve started to speak.

Steve explained everything they had been through to stop the terrorist cell. He told of finding Lizzie's lifeless body tied to the bed. He spoke of the condition in which they found her. Emma clutched Michael closer. She couldn't believe they were too late. They were so confident they would get to her in time. Rob had just heard her the day before. What could have happened to her that killed her that quickly? She had read of older couples losing a spouse. Once that happened, it wasn't long until the spouse who remained died of a broken heart. Did they kill her? Did they starve her to death? Did she die of dehydration?

"How did she die?" she asked, looking up to Michael for the answer.

"We won't know until they finish with the autopsy," Michael replied.

Rob couldn't take anymore, he had to leave the room. He made his way to his bedroom and dove face first onto the bed he had shared with his Lizzie.

He gathered her pillow close and inhaled her scent. It smelled like Lizzie, uniquely her. He sobbed into her pillow, holding it close to his face. His pleas for release from the pain were so strong, no noise escaped his throat. He took her scent for granted every single day, and now he would never smell her again. He bartered with God to allow him to hold Lizzie one more time. Just one more time, and then he would accept that she was dead. He could let her go if he got to hold her one more time.

He eventually cried himself to sleep.

Downstairs with Michael seated at the kitchen table, Emma kneeled in front of him much the same way he had once kneeled in front of her. She gently dabbed the dried blood from Michael's face with a warm washcloth.

"Are you going to tell me how this happened?" she asked, agitated at how Michael was once again keeping her in the dark. He didn't like to talk about himself, that much was clear, but she needed to know what had happened. Had a terrorist got a hold of him?

"You won't like the answer, and I don't want you thinking less of him," Michael responded, meeting Emma's determined crystal blue eyes. "He's my best friend."

"What? Rob did this to you? Why?" she asked, furious that Rob would lay a hand on him.

"You don't understand, Emma," Michael said, stroking her face with the backside of his fingers, trying to ease her mental state.

"Try me. I'm real good at understanding."

"He blamed you and me for what happened to Lizzie. He wanted an outlet for his anguish. I was there. He didn't do anything to me I didn't let happen."

Her misty eyes met his. "Why does he think that? I stole all of the information from my employer to save Lizzie. Why would he think we were to blame for Lizzie's death?" she rambled.

"Because we saved you first." Michael exhaled the secret, hoping Emma would not start blaming herself. He was doing enough of that for the both of them.

Tears streamed down her face. She felt for Rob, but she couldn't bring herself to understand how he could hurt his best friend. "So, you look like this because of me," she muttered.

He met her gaze with determination. "It is not because of you. Do not think, for one second, we would have done anything differently. We had to save you. I could never let anything happen to you. The way I feel about you, Emma, doesn't make sense, but I feel it nonetheless."

"But Lizzie died because you were saving me," she cried, lowering her head into Michael's lap. She left her head there, turned to the side, torturing Michael with her tears.

Michael cradled her head and stroked her hair. "No, Lizzie died because of what the terrorists did to her. It wasn't because of you. You were only trying to help her, just like I was. But Rob needed to take out the pain he was feeling on someone. I was there. I'm his best friend. I understand how he works, so I let myself be his punching bag. I'll heal. I'll heal a lot sooner than he will. He'll feel the loss of Lizzie for a long time to come. Look at me," he said, grabbing her chin and forcing her cloudy blue eyes to his. "You are not to blame for Lizzie's death. I won't have it. There was nothing we could have done to save her. God knows we tried. We just got there too late."

"Yeah, because you were too busy saving me. I'll never forgive myself, Michael. Never."

Michael felt lost. What could he do to convince her it wasn't her fault? Although he felt guilty himself, he would never blame her.

He rationalized out loud for both their sakes. "Look. I would never have met you if it wasn't for the terrorists threatening Rob with Lizzie's life. I would never have come to your home and tried to kidnap you. We would never have had to steal the documents and prototype. We wouldn't have had to save you if the terrorists hadn't hired me to kidnap you. This all leads back to the terrorists. I need you to see that."

She parted his knees by leaning into him. She needed to feel he didn't blame her. It was bad enough she blamed herself. She leaned in and pressed her lips softly to Michael's. Michael pressed his tongue against her lips, asking for entrance. She parted her lips, and he gently stroked at her bottom lip. She tasted his guilt and his pain. She felt the depths of his feelings for her, and she tried to communicate the same. Their tender kiss lasted until Tony entered the room, excusing himself with a cough.

Emma and Michael looked at him with a look of contentment in their eyes and tear tracks staining their faces.

"Are you hungry?" Tony asked, not waiting for an answer. "Steve is. I can make something. Breakfast ingredients are all Rob has left," Tony said.

Michael was starving. He couldn't remember the last time he ate.

Tony placed the scrambled eggs and bacon on the table. Michael served Emma bacon, and she looked at him coyly from hooded lashes. Then he served himself. Although it was difficult for Michael to eat, he managed to get the food over his lips and into his stomach.

It was 0800 hours when Tony announced, "All the arrangements have been made. Her parents are driving down today, but they're staying at the Hampton Inn in town."

"Good. There isn't enough room at my house, and I can't bear the thought of having to face them right now," Rob replied. "I 'm having a hard enough time making it through the day, and it just started."

Rob hadn't cried since his mother arrived the day before. Having her there helped him a great deal. She cooked and cleaned and took care of him just like she did when he was younger. Of course, he was her baby. He could always lean on her, and lean on her he did.

"It's only been two days, man. Cut yourself some slack. You suffered a great loss. I can't even begin to imagine how you feel," Tony said.

"I feel empty," Rob offered. "I feel like I have no reason to live."

"Don't talk like that. You have your mother and five brothers who will kick your ass for even hearing you say that," Tony countered.

"I know man. I just don't know how I am going to get through tomorrow."

"We'll all be there with you. You're not alone," Tony assured him.

"I'm sorry, Tony, but you have no idea how this feels," Rob said, dejected.

Tony walked across the room to Rob and threw his arms around the man. He held him close and tight like the tough son-of-a-bitch Tony knew him to be. Tony lent him his strength, and Rob soaked up every ounce.

Upstairs, Emma wriggled closer to Michael's back. He had his arm draped around her mid-section, careful not to touch her healing wound. Michael had a few cuts on his eyebrow and lip, but they were closed and healing. He had some nasty looking bruises on his face that, in all honesty, looked a lot worse than they felt. Unless someone touched them, he could forget about them.

Emma was rewarded with his stiff erection pressed against her butt. She pushed in closer. It felt like forever since the last time they'd been intimate with each other. The last two days had been about healing physically, and helping Rob cope with his loss. Now she craved Michael. She hungered for him with an ache deep in her core. She needed to feel him enter her and possess her again.

She rolled in his arms until she was facing him. She pressed up against his hard body and was rewarded with a low growl that escaped his throat. He rubbed up against her belly with his erection. She met him with equal force. Without saying a word, she gently stroked his eyebrow and ran her finger down his face. She leaned in and pressed her lips to his sensitive neck. She felt him shudder at her touch. He pulled her closer to him until every part of her touched him. She tangled her legs with his and nipped at his neck. He hummed his approval in her ear. He nibbled at her earlobe, causing her to purr in satisfaction. She ran her fingers through his chest hair down to his happy trail. She wanted to make love to Michael. She didn't want him to take her fast and hard. This time she wanted slow and strong.

She traced the center line of his chest lazily with her nails, causing chills to spread throughout his body. He coveted her with the deepest part of his being. He wanted to feel her tight core sheathe his hungry member. He leaned up on his elbow and cradled the back of her head with his hand. He brought her mouth closer to his and kissed her with a passion he had never known.

Emma moaned into his mouth at the feel of his lips pressed against hers, so soft and inviting. She could easily get lost in his kiss. She felt a tingle start at the top of her spine and spread downward. Goose bumps rose on her skin. She felt lightheaded. He left her breathless.

He removed his boxer briefs and tossed them onto the floor. He then helped her wiggle out of her panties, pulling them down her legs, trailing with his fingertips as he went. He wanted to do more than please her. He wanted her to remember this morning for the rest of her life. He slowly dragged his fingertips back up her legs in a methodical manner. When he reached the apex of her thighs, he spread her folds and gently applied pressure in a circular fashion to her throbbing nub while he leaned in to nip and then kiss her neck.

Emma leaned her head back to allow him greater access. She ran her hands up and down, palming the large muscles in his arms. She gently caressed his face as he made love to her with his mouth. She arched under his touch. She was aching from the gift he was bestowing upon her with his fingers.

Michael dipped his hand lower and slightly crooked two fingers. He pushed inside her entrance, and she moaned loudly at the intrusion. She was so wet, he longed to taste her juices, but this morning was all about her. He easily and slowly slid two fingers in and out of her, rubbing his thumb against her clit. He was worshipping at his temple, learning everything he could. He would always bring her pleasure before he sought his own.

He took his time, exploring her body. She had never had anyone take this kind of time learning her body before. She reached the edge of her orgasm as he continued to slide his fingers in and out of her body. She climbed higher until she reached the height of pleasure. Her orgasm overtook her. She shuddered, and her legs trembled. She burst into tiny shards of light as she arched her head back and called out his name.

Hearing his name torn from her lips was more than Michael could bear. He was close just watching her receive his pleasure. The way her body responded to his amazed him. He had never been with a woman who was so responsive to his every touch. The way she trembled told him she had achieved her orgasm. He lay on top of her, bracing himself with his forearms so he could look into her beautiful, electric eyes. "Keep your eyes open. I want to watch you," he said as he positioned himself at her entrance.

He was careful to work her back up, rubbing the head against her nub. He moved back and forth against her, applying pressure. In no time, she was begging for him to enter her. "Michael, please. I want to feel you inside me."

He leaned forward and kissed her gently as he slid into her. They both moaned. He pulled out slowly and drove back into her while he kissed her shoulder and then her neck, finally making his way back to her lips. She parted her lips and opened her mouth to allow his tongue access. He thrust his tongue inside her mouth with the same controlled movements he was making into her core. She sucked on his tongue the same way her body sucked at his cock. He was in a state of bliss. He drove into her slow and steady, just the way she needed. Her hands roamed his back, massaging his muscles. He caressed her face with his hand, gently stroking her cheek. He gazed into her eyes as he entered her. Their eyes connected, communicating all of the love and trust neither one could voice. His strong and steady thrusts brought her closer to the edge. She met each thrust, rubbing her pelvis against his pubic bone. The stimulation was too much.

He had to hold on. He picked up the pace, still going slow and steady, but he was driving into her harder and harder with each thrust.

"I'm there," she moaned.

"Stay with me, baby. Come with me," he admonished as he thrust into her again, this time harder than the last.

They shattered into pieces together. His hot liquid pulsed into her tight center as her pulsating labia sucked greedily at his member.

Falling from grace, he rested himself against her body. Flesh to flesh, nothing stood between them but unspoken words. When should he tell her how he felt? Would she reciprocate the feelings? He was in love with her. He needed to convince her he was worthy of her love before he confessed. Unrequited love was not an option. He had to find a way to get to her heart. He had to enmesh himself as deeply in her heart as she was in his.

"Stay right there. I want to clean you up," he commanded as he peeked out of the door making sure the coast was clear for his naked body.

He went into the bathroom and wet a washcloth with warm water. He returned to Emma as quickly as possible. He dipped the washcloth between her legs and cleaned the mixture of their pleasure from between her thighs.

"I'd like nothing more than to stay in here all day with you," he said, smiling at her lovely face.

"I'd like that too," she said, returning his smile.

"But we have to be there for Rob. We'll have plenty of time, just you and me, once the funeral is over," he assured her.

She was taken aback by his plans. He planned on keeping her around after the funeral, and she was out of danger. Her smile brightened reaching her eyes.

"To what do I owe the pleasure of that smile?" he asked, a quizzical look upon his face.

"You said 'after the funeral.' I thought we wouldn't be together after the funeral. You know, you'd go your way. I'd go mine," she responded.

Michael immediately tensed. She thought she was leaving him after the funeral. That couldn't happen. Surely her smile was not an I'm-happy-to-see-you-go kind of smile. It was now or never.

"Do you like what just happened between us?" he questioned, tensing, waiting for her response.

"Michael, what I just experienced was mind-blowing. I have never had a lover like you," she replied, a Cheshire grin still on her face.

"Is that all you think we are, lovers?" he asked, dreading her answer.

"What are you trying to say?" she questioned. She wasn't going to make a fool out of herself and say anything before he said something first. This was the first *where are we going* conversation they had. She wasn't going to be the one to ruin it.

"I can't speak for you, Emma. But I've told you, on more than one occasion, that you're mine," he stated, trying to gauge her reaction.

She had thought he said that in the throes of pleasure. She could see now he really meant it. She felt a wave of relief wash over her body. She visibly relaxed into the bed. He moved closer to her, needing to caress her face as he said the next words. He cupped her face in his hands and looked directly into her eyes. "I want to find out where this can take us, because I am not letting you go. Not now. Not ever," he alleged.

She was dumbstruck. He was taking forever. What did he mean? Surely not *forever,* forever.

"I want to see where we can go, too, Michael," she said as she watched him noticeably exhale. "I was afraid to say anything because I thought this was all about the adrenaline rush for you. I thought once everything was over, we would go back to our separate lives."

"Let me make myself perfectly clear, so there is no room for confusion. You. Are. Mine. We do not have separate lives any longer. I want to be with you every day, in every way. We don't have to rush anything. We have all the time in the world. I want you comfortable with the fact that I am not letting you go anytime soon, unless, of course, that is what you want. Is that what you want?" he questioned, sadness clouding his eyes.

"Of course not, Michael. I want to be yours. I love the way that sounds, and more importantly, I love the way that feels," she reassured him, taking his face into her hands.

She brought her lips to his, but this time, she did the taking. She brought her mouth over his in a reverent kiss. She didn't want any doubts left in that gorgeous head of his.

"You don't mean to control me, do you, Michael?" she asked afraid of the answer.

"Only to keep you safe. And in the bedroom," he said with a devilish grin.

She grinned back, gazing into his light eyes, which were now so full of life. She never remembered a time when his eyes shined the way they did at that exact moment. He had said it to her after having sex, which meant he wasn't just trying to charm his way into her bed. He had said it, and he had meant it.

"I'll be going back to work, Michael. My career is very important to me, and I have to finish what I started," she said, determined not to budge on this issue.

"Of course, you are. I would never want to keep you from anything that makes you happy. Because, Emma, that's all I want, a happy you," he said, leaning in to kiss her once more.

"Good. You make me so happy, Michael," she admitted.

"We probably should get downstairs and have some breakfast. You can give a man an appetite," he bantered.

"I know what you mean." She winked.

CLOSER

Emma sat on the couch waiting for the guys to share two bathrooms. Today was the day of the funeral. It was a good day for a funeral. The skies were dark and overcast on the verge of rain. However, the weatherman said the chance of rain was only twenty percent.

"I just got an email of the autopsy report," Rob said, handing the printed paper to Michael. "I can't read it. Will you read it to me?" Rob whispered.

"Do you want to go into another room, someplace private?" Michael asked, cognizant of Rob's need for privacy.

Rob looked determined. "Nope. You can read it to everyone here. Everyone here had a hand in attempting to save Lizzie. Everyone here can know."

"Immediate cause of death—due to internal bleeding from repeated physical and sexual trauma, and dehydration," Michael read from the report. "Manner of death—Homicide. Remarks—Decedent presented as homicide victim. Presence of antemortem bruising on lower abdomen and back consistent with internal examination and indicative of internal bleeding from trauma to reproductive organs. Lab values showed hypernatremia indicative of dehydration in addition to hypovolemia from trauma."

"Fuck," Rob cried, "she suffered."

"There wasn't that much blood on the mattress. What does it mean?" asked Michael.

"It means those bastards raped her to death. They tore her reproductive organs during the rapes, causing blood to leak out of the vessels and into the surrounding tissue. The bruises on her body would only form if she were alive while she bled out. It means she fucking suffered. They tortured her to death with rape." Rob could taste the bile rising in the back of his throat. He was going to be ill. He made a run for the downstairs bathroom and wretched up his breakfast.

"Rob, man, what can I do?" Michael asked as Rob reemerged from the bathroom.

Rob quickly lowered his head to keep from making eye contact with anybody in the room. He had the information now, but that only made things worse. Knowing how she had suffered was yet a lower level of hell for Rob.

Emma started to cry. She cried for Rob and for Lizzie. She cried because if she hadn't been working on the project, the terrorist would have never wanted her.

Michael sensed the direction of her thoughts and found her in three long strides. He wrapped her in his arms and repeated, "It wasn't your fault."

She had no idea Lizzie had suffered such torture. She would never forgive the terrorists, and she thought if they weren't already dead or in custody, she would kill them herself. For the first time since meeting Michael, she finally understood why Michael laughed the day he described the torture he was going to inflict on Ahmed. She understood the will to inflict pain.

Sympathy filled the men's eyes. They may not know exactly what Rob was going through, but they felt his pain. He could tell. Their collective strength gave Rob the power to walk out the door.

At the funeral home, there was a steady stream of mourners wishing to pay their respects to Lizzie. The casket was open, and the funeral director had done a nice job fixing Lizzie up the best he could. Rob had chosen her favorite blue sundress, even though it was winter. Summer was Lizzie's favorite time of year.

One-by-one, the mourners hugged Rob and Lizzie's parents, who stood to the side of the open casket. Rob couldn't keep his eyes off his Lizzie. He longed to hold her in his arms, and he would after everyone had left him alone. The mourners knelt before the casket, saying their last prayers, wishing Lizzie a peaceful afterlife. Some even prayed she find her way back to them in her next life.

Once the mourners left to make their way to the cemetery, Rob asked for a few minutes alone with his Lizzie. Everyone hugged him again and left. Rob went to the casket and picked up a very stiff Lizzie in his arms. He stroked the hair off her forehead. She wouldn't like the haircut the funeral director gave her. Rob held her for what felt like only a few minutes before laying her carefully back down.

"You were it for me, Lizzie," he sobbed at her side. "I will never love again. No woman could ever replace you. I don't know how I am supposed to go on without you. Could you give me some sign? Tell me what you want me to do because, Lizzie, all I can think about is joining you."

The aroma of the room full of flowers filled his nostrils, and he was immediately taken back to the time they spent together in the tropics. He remembered the way she looked in her bikini, lying out on the white sand, so full of life. He remembered chasing her into the crystal blue waters and throwing her into the air. He remembered the way they made love every night under the stars. He knew the memories were Lizzie's way of asking him to remember the good times. And their life together was filled with them. His memories were a stark contrast to the girl who rested in the casket. It was his Lizzie, no doubt, but her essence was gone. He sobbed some more.

When his sobs slowed and he was able to catch his breath, he slowly slipped his dog tags from around his neck. It was all that he had that meant anything to him. He placed the metal tags around her neck and lowered her head back to the pillow. He was leaving a piece of his heart in that casket, the largest piece. He knew he would never get it back.

At the cemetery, he watched in a daze, not hearing a word the preacher said. Instead, he focused on all of his memories with Lizzie. He remembered the last time they grilled steaks. He focused on how she could bring fun to anything, even cooking. What was he to do now? As they lowered the casket into the ground, Rob fell to his knees. He wanted nothing more than to join her.

His brothers knew he needed this time to grieve for his loss. The stood by at the ready, as a source of constant emotional support for Rob. Someone would have to stay with him over the course of the next several weeks, and Michael hoped Steve was up for the mission.

Once back at the house, the mourners gathered, ate the catered food, and drank the drinks provided by Rob's mother. She made her rounds, talking to each guest, asking them to share a fond memory of Lizzie. She wanted Rob to hear the good that Lizzie brought to life.

Rob was too busy burying himself under four fingers of scotch. He was on his fourth drink by the time most of the mourners left.

"Emma and I are taking off tomorrow, but Steve said he will hang around and keep you company for a while," Michael told Rob.

Rob's hazy eyes met Michael's. *Was he even hearing Michael?*

"I'm only an hour away. If you need me, call, and I'll come right away. It's just, I think you need us out of your hair," he explained to his brother.

Now that he had Emma and she agreed to be his, all he wanted to do was touch her, and he knew Rob didn't need to see that. He didn't need to see them so happy around each other. They were mourning for Rob and Lizzie now. But, eventually, they would move on, and he didn't know how long it would take Rob to do the same.

He felt confident in his decision to keep Steve there. Steve said he didn't have any jobs lined up. Tony and Rob didn't exactly see eye-to-eye after their last mission, but he was impressed with the way they seemed to bury the hatchet. Tony wouldn't be a good choice to stay because he had already said he had two jobs lined up. Kevin worked for Homeland Security and had a wife. And Michael had just found Emma. Steve said he could afford to stay for three weeks. That should be enough time to get Rob through the worst of it. Still, Michael was worried that Rob no longer had anything to live for, that he would end his own life.

They rented a car to drive back to Emma's cabin. It was an uneventful drive, but night had fallen. They would return the rental car in the morning. Tonight was about them. Emma cooked pork chops smothered in gravy, complete with mashed potatoes and green beans. He could get used to her cooking. The meat fell from the bone and melted in his mouth. If he didn't love this woman before, he did now.

After dinner, she opened a bottle of white wine. She liked drinking a good Chardonnay to relax and after the last week and a half, she needed to unwind. She strolled into the living room and was gifted with a fire burning bright in her fireplace. How she missed her cabin. For a while there, she thought she would never see it again. She stopped at the edge of the sofa and handed Michael a glass of wine. She sat next to him, and he put his arm around her shoulder, safely tucking her into his side. It was a protective gesture she adored.

"I'm going back to work tomorrow," she said, waiting for an argument.

"You're forgetting the friendly CIA agent still after you."

"I didn't forget about him, but I can't live my life in fear. Besides, I work at a high security facility. No one will be getting past Paul," she asserted.

"Is it absolutely imperative that you go in?" Michael asked cautiously. He didn't want her upset with him because of his controlling ways.

"I now have less than two weeks to work out the bugs with the prototype. That is, assuming Homeland Security returned it," she said dejectedly.

"Let me call Kevin," he said reaching into his pants pocket for his phone.

Kevin answered on the second ring. "Did you get home okay?" Kevin asked, still concerned about Ingrams himself.

"We did. We're at the cabin. She's safe for now. Listen, I'm calling to make sure Homeland returned Emma's project to the DOD?" Michael asked, waiting for an affirmative response. Kevin didn't disappoint.

"We did three days ago. How's Rob doing?" Kevin asked.

"We had to leave so Rob wasn't reminded of what he had with Lizzie. Honestly, I'm worried he's gonna try to take his own life."

Emma gently squeezed his hand in a reassuring gesture.

"I asked Steve to stay with him for the next couple of weeks. I figured the next few weeks would be the hardest," Michael explained.

"How did Rob take to that idea?" Kevin asked.

Michael looked into Emma's eyes and said, "I didn't really give him a choice."

Kevin started laughing on the other end of the phone. Boy, was it good to hear laughter.

"What's so funny?" Michael asked in mock horror.

"You. There you go, imposing your will on others. How is Emma gonna take that?" Kevin asked.

Michael smiled. "You let me worry about Emma." Michael squeezed Emma's hand this time. The men talked for a few more minutes before Michael disconnected the call.

"Everything has been returned to your office. Homeland informed the powers that be of the situation, so you won't be in any trouble for removing the documents or the prototype. Paul was left out of the loop, so everything should go back to the way it was before with him. Homeland told only those on a need-to-know basis, which would be your immediate supervisor, the general, and the agents at the CIA," Michael explained.

"What are we going to do about Ingrams? We have no proof," she said. Now that she had time to relax, she had time to think. She was almost healed from the beating she had suffered at his hands. Just the thought of his name raised the hair on the back of her neck.

"Ingrams isn't finished yet. He is a man with a vendetta against you and, now, me. He will stop at nothing to rid the world of both of us. We'll just have to be prepared. If you really want to go back to work tomorrow, I'll drive you to and from your office. I'll escort you into and out of the building. At no times, and under no circumstances, are you to be alone or leave the building without me," he commanded.

"What about my usual lunch with Bethany? She'll get suspicious if I don't meet her at least once at the deli," Emma clarified.

"The only way this is going to work is if you don't leave the building without me. Pack your lunch and make up some excuse Bethany will believe," he said, allowing no room for argument. It was his way or no way. "This is only temporary. We have to handle Agent Ingrams, and then all will go back to normal," he said, smiling, hoping to ease the constraints he was putting on her.

She got a worried look in her eye. "All will go back to normal? As in you and me will go back to normal?" she asked.

"Yes. Everything will return to the way it was before," he answered.

Her eyes started to tear up. She looked up at him with a sadness that touched his soul. Of course, why didn't he mind his words better? "Your daily life will go back to normal with one difference." He reached down and kissed her passionately on the lips. When he broke the kiss, he said, "Me."

He cupped her face in his hands and wiped the tears away with his large thumbs. He took her mouth again in a fierce, possessive kiss. Passion overtook them. Their hands searched out bare skin. Their mouths found places to nip and lick. He stripped her of her defenses and then removed his own.

Michael laid her down on the rug in front of the fireplace. He drew a line in-between her breasts down to her clit and back up again. He was driving her wild with the way he was caressing her. "Are you wet for me?" he asked, moving his fingers down to her opening to find out for himself.

"You do have that effect on me," she quipped, then quickly gasped as he pushed two fingers inside her. He made the come hither sign with his fingers and stroked the front wall of her pussy.

"Oh my god, Michael. What are you doing? That feels incredible," she moaned.

"Then I've found just what I was looking for," he bantered. "That, my love, is your g-spot."

"Whatever it is, don't stop."

He continued stroking inside her, adding pressure to her clit with his thumb. For each push in, he would circle and push against her clit. He had her squirming from his touch. She was thrusting her hips into the air to get closer.

She reached for the rug and grabbed it between her fingers. He expertly brought her to climax. The world dissolved. She melted into the soft, plush carpet at her back. It was an intense orgasm that left her strung out. He continued to play with her, but she was sensitive. She tried pushing his hand away, but he wouldn't budge. Finally, he brought his hands up to her nipples, running his thumbs over the buds. He lowered his head and sucked one into his mouth, sucking it and nipping at her. He had an expert mouth. His hand cupped her other breast and pinched her nipple. When he released his mouth, he moved to give the other breast the same attention. His hand traveled back down to her center. This time, when he touched her clit, she moaned. He dipped his finger inside her core and brought it to his mouth. She watched as he sucked her juices from his finger. God he was erotic. He lifted her leg and placed it on his shoulder. He straddled her other leg.

At her entrance, and knowing she was wet and ready, he thrust inside of her to ease his craving. She was like a drug to him. He didn't just want. No, he *needed* to be inside her. He worked her over, thrusting in and out. He threw her leg down and switched angles. He thrust harder and harder.

"I want you with me this time, Michael," she groaned as she ascended higher. "Say you're with me."

Her words were his undoing. "I'm with you."

They came together. She dissolved into him. She would never get close enough to him.

They had made love on the rug in front of the crackling fire—one of her fantasies. Once they both came back to center, they made their way, hand-in-hand, to her bedroom where they slept soundly in each other's arms.

The next morning, Emma awoke to the smell of fresh coffee. She gingerly got out of bed and walked into her bathroom. She showered, brushed her teeth, and dried her hair, leaving it falling loosely at her shoulders. She dressed in a pencil skirt with a fitted cream colored silk button-down blouse. Then she walked down the hallway to find Michael.

Michael sat at the kitchen counter drinking his coffee. He got up and met her as she entered the kitchen. He kissed her gently on the lips. "Good morning, baby," he said, grinning from ear to ear. "You look mighty fine this morning."

She returned his smile. "I'm excited to get back to work. I really want to work out the bugs on the Hummingbird and finish the project on time," she explained, still in his arms.

She moved past him to the coffee pot to fill a mug. "I want to leave after my second cup. Will you be ready to take me then?" she asked, hope filling her chest.

"I'm ready now if you want," Michael said, smacking her luscious behind with his hand.

"Michael," she admonished.

She walked over to the bar and sat in her usual seat. She started thumbing through the stack of mail that had piled up in her mailbox, which Michael had retrieved for her that morning. She paused halfway through the stack, a look of fear crossing her features, which had been radiant a few seconds ago.

"What is it?" Michael asked, reaching for the envelope that had caught her attention.

"It's from the CIA, Lewiston branch, and it is hand-addressed to me," she whispered as she handed the letter to Michael.

Michael inspected the front of the letter and nothing stood out. Then he used his index finger to rip open the envelope. He pulled out the folded letter. He read: *"You managed to escape last time. Next time, you won't be so lucky. I know all about your boyfriend. It is amazing what a few words entered into the right database can produce. Please tell Michael I look forward to our next encounter."* The letter wasn't signed, and it was typed and printed on plain computer paper. Nothing about the letter would appear threatening to anyone but them.

"It's from Ingrams, isn't it?" Emma asked cautiously.

Michael nodded his head and handed her the letter. She read it. She felt sweat start to form at her temples. What were they going to do? Ingrams knew where she lived, and he knew all about Michael.

How did Ingrams plan on killing them? She didn't want to think about it. She had to continue on with her day the best she could, and that involved getting to her high security office building. She finished her second cup of coffee and asked, "Are you ready?"

Suddenly the cheer and comfort she felt waking with Michael this morning left her. Project Hummingbird felt more and more like a burden, which was getting too heavy to carry. She knew Ingrams wasn't playing with a full deck, and she had no idea when he would strike. He had complete access to top secret databases and information through the CIA. He also had resources. He was able to get her to a cabin in the middle of a national park and had access to a boat. If Michael hadn't saved her, she would be shark meat. Snap out of it, she told herself.

Michael was there in a stride, comforting her, reassuring her. "I won't let anything happen to you. I promise." He smiled, but it didn't reach his eyes. He ran his fingers up and down her arms.

She wanted to believe him, to trust him. He had saved her once from Ingrams, but he couldn't prevent Ingrams from taking her or beating her. Could he stop Ingrams this time?

"I know what you're thinking," Michael said, looking straight ahead, unable to make eye contact with her. The guilt he felt was too much. He forced himself to meet her frightened eyes. "You're thinking I couldn't save you the first time. How am I going to save you this time?" He moved away from her, turning his back. Looking into those scared, blank eyes was more than he could stand.

"Actually," she said as she walked up to him and hugged his body from behind, "I was thinking about how you saved me last time. If you hadn't shown up, he would've killed me." She squeezed him tighter. He placed his hands over hers.

"Thank you for saying that, but I should have never let him take you in the first place," Michael admitted.

"Nonsense. He would have killed me in your car if you didn't. Letting him take me gave you a chance to save my life." It was her turn to reassure him. She stood on her tip toes and kissed the back of his neck.

He turned in her arms and was surprised to find strength and resolve in her eyes. What he didn't find was blame. He felt like a weight had been lifted from his chest and he could finally breathe again. He exhaled as he moved closer to her lips. He hesitated for a moment, lingering, feeling her breath against his. Time stood still. A million thoughts rushed through his head, but the one that helped him was her belief in him. He leaned a little closer and touched her lips with his.

"Let's get going. I have a lot to get done today," she said, turning to grab her purse from the counter.

They put on their coats and made their way to the driveway. Both the rental car and her Subaru were parked next to the back door. He walked her to her car. After three strides arm in arm with Emma, he stopped her.

"Wait!" he said as he peered down at the ground. "When is the last time you were at your car?" he asked.

"The day you arrived at my house. Why?" she asked, following his eyes to the ground.

There, visible in the packed snow, were a set of large footprints leading to the car. "Someone was here." He pointed to the footprints on the ground. "And they did something to your car. Look," he said as they followed the tracks to the driver's side of her SUV. "There is something under the car." He looked straight into her eyes, expressing his fear for her safety and his love for her being.

"How could you possibly know that?" she asked, hoping he was wrong.

"Do you see that print there?" He pointed next to her car door. "Those are knee prints. Somebody planted something under your car." He knelt down beside her car door. "Go in the house until I tell you it's safe."

She didn't want to leave him alone to find whatever it was planted under her car. *First the letter from Ingrams and now . . . .*

"It's a homemade pipe bomb," he growled, lying flat on his back, his neck straining at an awkward angle to see under the car.

"A bomb?" She stared at him wide-eyed.

The spark of life that had returned only a few minutes ago was now gone. It was replaced with horror. Her face froze at the impact of Michael's words, which hit her like a piano falling from the sky. "Can you disarm it?" she asked, afraid of his answer.

"Yes," he said confidently. "But I need a mirror. Do you have a hand-held mirror?" he asked.

"On my dresser," was all she could manage. She stood frozen in place. It was so cold it looked like she was exhaling cigarette smoke. She hadn't put on her gloves. She was regretting that choice now. She placed her hands into her pockets, watching in horror as Michael's head lay underneath the bomb. She willed herself not to tremble. She didn't know exactly what would set off the bomb, and she was deathly afraid of losing Michael.

"Get inside now and get me that mirror," he demanded, leaving no room for argument.

She went inside the house and shut the door.

Who would plant a car bomb? The terrorists were dead, so that only left Ingrams. It had to be Ingrams. He knew where she lived. He had sent the letter. He probably didn't know about the terrorist cell being out of play. He probably thought he could make it look like the GIA.

How complicated was the device? Michael had told her he worked with explosives in the Army. Thank God for small miracles. He said he could disarm it.

Why was she still questioning if she could trust him? They both had confessed feelings for each other. Was something so inherently wrong with her that she couldn't even trust the man she loved?

She returned with her grandmother's pearl-inlaid hand mirror.

"Here's the mirror," she said as she placed it in his hands. His hand looked extra rough juxtaposed to the delicate mirror.

"Get back in the house," he grunted.

She didn't want to disobey that voice. She ran back into the house and peered out the kitchen door window.

He lowered himself back down until he was lying on the ground. He angled the mirror to see exactly what type of homemade device he was working with. If he didn't know better, he would say the terrorists planted it. It was a dirty bomb, exactly up their alley. He found what he was looking for—the 9 volt battery. The air was extremely cold, yet he found himself wiping sweat from his brow. He had done this a hundred times in the Army, but this time was different. This time it wasn't just himself or his brothers at risk. This time it was the love of his life.

The muscles of his neck strained at an awkward angle to see the power source. He couldn't make a mistake, not with Emma's life at stake. Carefully, so as to not touch any part of the bomb, he popped the power source from its housing. Confident he had disarmed it, he stood back up, brushing the snow from his clothes. He didn't feel the cold that had settled into his bones. He was more concerned about removing the bomb from her car. He didn't have his car, so he didn't have the tools he needed. He said a silent prayer and then placed his hand on the car's door handle.

Emma peered at him through her kitchen window, and their eyes met. She willed him not to die.

"I'm going to open the door," Michael said.

She squeezed her eyes shut again and held her breath as he lifted the handle and slowly opened the door. After a few seconds, nothing happened. She peeked at him with one eye. Once the door was the entire way open, she raced out of the kitchen and flung herself into his arms. She had never been so frightened to lose another human being in her life. They stood in the cold February morning air, wrapped in each other's arms. Tears of relief flooded her eyes. She hugged him tighter. He was her savior, her protector. She couldn't remember what her life was like before he broke into her home, and she didn't want to.

CHAPTER
TWENTY-NINE

They arrived at her office building in the rental car a little later than Emma would have liked. Always the gentleman, Michael hopped out of the car and raced around to her side to get the door for her. He extended the crook of his arm. She placed her arm through it and was escorted into her office building.

They stood just inside the doors of the lobby. Michael looked around the modern building. The security guard was stationed at a desk separating the lobby from the rest of the first floor. There was even a decorative koi pond with a waterfall, serving as a barrier to the rest of the floor. The soft sound of the falling water was rather soothing. He wondered if it was placed there to deter questions about what really went on upstairs.

"I programmed my number into your phone. Call me when you're ready to leave." He bent his head to give her a kiss on the lips.

She was a little shy about such a public display of affection, especially at her place of employment. But once his lips met hers, she melted into his touch. She forgot about the people in the building. She forgot about the cameras. She forgot about Paul watching her.

He had that effect on her. She had never wanted anyone with the intensity with which she wanted him, and all it took was a kiss. "Let's go back home," she said with a devilish grin.

"What kind of boyfriend would I be if I let you play hooky with me, especially when I know how important finishing your project is to you?" he asked, playfully nipping at her bottom lip.

She groaned. He was right.

"You're mine. Remember that, Emma. Let me hear you say it," he said before releasing his hold on her body.

"I'm yours," she professed with a knowing smile. Tonight was only a few hours away. She would just have to wait.

He released her and said, "Have a good day, Emma. Remember: call me. Do not leave this building without me."

She didn't need his reminder. After this morning, she would do whatever he said.

She'd been gone from work so long, she was incredibly behind on her project. The Hummingbird dominated her thoughts as she made her way to the security desk.

"Hi, Paul," she said, blushing, and handed over her purse and cell phone.

"I missed you around here, girl. Where have you been?" he asked, trying to avoid eye contact after just witnessing her kiss with Michael.

This was it. She had to get good at lying and quick. "I have had a terrible case of the flu. I didn't want to risk spreading it to anyone." The lie rolled off of her tongue smoother than she thought it sounded.

"Well, I am sure glad to see you back and feeling better, Ms. Welby," Paul replied.

"Thank you, Paul. It's good to be back," she said with a smile as she started to make her way around the desk to the entrance.

She pulled out her security card and swiped it through the reader. The green light indicated she could proceed. She made her way to the stairs and swiped her card again. Again, the green light. Truth be told, she was nervous her card would no longer work. Whatever Homeland said to her bosses, it must have done the trick, because she was walking upstairs to her fourth floor office. She pulled the door open, and the welcoming hum of busy workers filled her ears. She walked with a false sense of confidence to her lab. No one had stopped her yet. That must be a good sign.

She'd been buried in her project when her phone buzzed with an incoming text: *I'm sitting here with my hand on my cock, thinking about all the things I'm going to do to you tonight.*

She blinked in surprise. She had never talked dirty with anyone before in her life, but with Michael, she found it turned her on. She certainly never sent naughty text messages.

She texted back: *I wish my hand was on your cock.* She hit the send button before she could change her mind.

Michael: *I can't wait to be buried inside your pussy.*

Emma: *I can't wait to feel your cock push into me for the first time.*

His words were undoing her there in her office. She felt that emptiness in her belly, the emptiness only Michael could fill. She grew moist between her legs, and he had only said two things to her. She had it bad for him. She needed relief from the ache he caused inside her. She squeezed her thighs together, hoping for some relief.

Emma: *I'm ready to go home. Please come and get me.*

Michael: *I'm outside waiting on the street. I will come into the lobby. Do not leave the building unless you are on my arm.*

She placed her files and notes back in her desk drawer. She put the Hummingbird back in its cage for the night. She would devote all of tomorrow to the project. She had a pretty clear understanding of the failure of the spray mechanism. Tomorrow she would fix it. Tonight, she wanted Michael. She put on her coat and walked to Bethany's office to say goodnight.

"I thought you'd be staying later. Then we could get some dinner tonight? Maybe a few drinks?" Bethany inquired.

"Sorry. I don't want to overdo it. I just got over being sick. Maybe this weekend?" she asked, hoping her friend would understand.

"Sure, sure. Although, I'm not sure which night I'll be available this weekend. I have another date with the guy from the club." She waved to her friend from behind her office desk.

"I'll see you tomorrow," Emma said as she hurried from the office and down the stairs to gather her things from Paul.

After a few minutes of small talk with Paul, she turned to see her gorgeous man waiting on her. She loved the way his unruly hair looked like a woman had just ran her hands through it, the way his dark eyelashes lined his eyes, the way his muscles bunched under his coat. She was all his, and she couldn't wait to get her hands on him.

Apparently, he must have felt the same, because as soon as she neared him, he pulled her to him and pressed his lips roughly to hers. It was a kiss filled with need, with desire. They stood in the lobby of the office building, kissing and touching each other. If she wasn't careful, this could end her career. She pulled back from his god-like form. "We have to at least leave the building, Michael," she admonished, absentmindedly touching her lips with her fingers.

She was burning inside for this man. She doubted they would make it home. They would probably have to pull over along the side of the road. She didn't think she could wait to ease the ache much longer. He extended his arm to her, and they walked out into the blustery late afternoon air.

Michael parked a few blocks down, so they had to walk into the wind. She looked up and noticed dark clouds gathering in the sky. The air felt charged with electricity, like a bad storm was coming. She snuggled into Michael's side to block the wind and give her some source of heat. She couldn't wait to get home, start a fire, drink hot chocolate, and make love all night.

A whole day without Michael and she was experiencing some serious withdrawals. The last time she was separated from him, he was risking his life to take down the terrorist cell and had come back to her badly beaten. What a difference several days made. He was on the mend and so was she. She hardly felt the sutures in her side any longer unless she stretched the wrong way. She no longer felt any pain, and she was thankful to Rob for taking such good care of her. If she would have had to go to the hospital, maybe Ingrams would have gotten to her all the sooner.

Thoughts of this morning plagued her mind. "Who do you think planted the bomb, Michael?" she asked, as they were still two blocks from the car.

"Well, the bomb itself was interesting. It was a classic terrorist homemade bomb. Something they can put together in no time at all. If I didn't kill those men with my own gun, I would say they're responsible. Whoever it was had to have the knowledge for that type of weapon," he said, lost in his thoughts.

"Do you think there are more terrorists out there after me?" She grimaced to think of the answer.

"I know there are more terrorists out there, but how would they know where you lived? Whoever did it knew not only knew where you lived, but they also knew you weren't home. They wouldn't risk getting caught. They would want to plant it when they knew no one was around. We were just damn lucky I walked you to your car this morning," he said.

She walked on as the sky grew darker, the wind biting through her skin. She reached her free hand into her pocket for warmth.

"Just one more block," he said. She wriggled closer to his body for warmth. He put his arm around her and pulled her into his side. She needed to be there, at his side. She was drawn to him like a plant to sunlight.

"Well, if it wasn't the terrorists, do you think it could have been Ingrams?" she asked.

"Honestly, I don't know. Ingrams seems like more of a hands-on type to me. It seemed like he wanted to get personal with you. A bomb is not something someone uses when they want a personal kill."

The way he could talk about killing like he did it every day of his life scared her, but she understood him now. She just hoped this nightmare would be over sooner rather than later.

They reached the car, and he opened her door. He rounded the car and got into the driver's seat. She reached for his leg. She lusted after him. She had to reassure herself he was really hers. She placed her hand on his thigh and slowly caressed it through his jeans.

At her touch, he went instantly hard. He grabbed her hand and placed it on his cock. "See what you do to me. No one has ever affected me the way you do."

She started to rub him through his jeans. The thought of having him inside her made her clit throb. A fire heated in her belly as her nipples strained against the lacy silk of her bra. Her silk shirt didn't do much to conceal the hard points of her breasts. He reached up and gently rolled one between his fingers.

"See what you do to me?" she cooed as she rubbed his cock with more pressure.

"I better get you home so I can take care of you." He groaned at the feel of her delicate hand on him.

He released her nipple, kissed her lips, and then started the car. They drove, her hand rubbing his cock the entire way to her apartment. They were staying in the city until Friday. It was already Wednesday, so a few nights in the city wouldn't hurt. Luckily, her apartment had a gas fireplace, so they still could have their fire.

He parked in the garage as she directed him to her spot. They walked hand-in-hand to the elevator. She pushed the button for the eighth floor. He took advantage of the time and kissed her like it was their last kiss. His hands found their way under her soft silk shirt to her breasts. He couldn't wait to see what she wore underneath because he wasn't there when she dressed that morning.

He cupped her breast as he kissed her and pushed her to the wall, pressing his bulging erection into her core. She molded to his body, her soft parts accommodating his hard parts. He managed to rub himself against her just as the elevator signaled their arrival on the eighth floor.

They walked down the hallway to her door. She could hear her keys jingling in her purse, but she couldn't find them. When she finally got her hands on them, Michael had nibbled and kissed her neck up and down twice. She quivered at his touch, but managed to unlock the door.

They entered her hallway. Even in the dim light, he was struck at how modern her apartment was. It was nothing like her cabin. It had clean lines and photographic landscape art, which adorned the walls in neat rows. Off of the long hallway was her kitchen. He followed her down the hallway into the living room. She flipped the switch, and the room flooded with light. He was watching her fine ass sway back and forth and didn't notice the man sitting in the chair with a gun pointed directly at his Emma.

CLOSER

Michael noticed her couch was red leather, just like the one at her cabin. But in this modern space, it took on a new feel. Everything about her apartment felt clinical. Like it was a showplace rather than a home.

"Good evening, Ms. Welby, Mr. Cartwright. I've been expecting you. I see you got the present I left for Ms. Welby." He indicated with his gun for them to enter the room and sit on the couch. "The weather forecast was calling for significant snow, which never came, or you would never have found my present, and my job here would be done."

Michael walked with Emma to the couch, and they sat down, clinging to each other.

"Oh, isn't that sweet? Two love birds." Ingrams pointed the gun directly at Emma's head. Michael knew he was trained and wouldn't miss if he fired. But why would he risk firing here? The gun didn't have a silencer on it.

"What do you want Ingrams? We took down the terrorist cell. Isn't that enough for you?" Michael asked, chin held high in defiance. He knew Ingrams harbored a grudge against the GIA.

"As a matter of fact, it is not enough for me, Mr. Cartwright. I want the engineer of Project Hummingbird dead. And now it looks like I'll have to kill you, too. Why did you get involved in this in the first place? I read your file. You were a good Green Beret. You even won the Medal of Honor for rescuing a village of women and children while you were in Afghanistan. Well, you and your team. I would certainly say that was 'above and beyond the call of duty,' Mr. Cartwright. How many children did you save because their fathers had abandoned them to join Al-Qaeda?" Ingrams asked with a look of respect for Michael in his eyes.

"That isn't the point. Why do you still want to harm Emma?" Michael asked, keeping his voice calm and even, which was no small task because he wanted to rip this fucker a new asshole. "What do you have against the GIA? We took down the cell that was in the U. S."

"There is more than one cell. Do you really think they're just going to give up on the idea of kidnapping your girlfriend? They won't stop until they obtain the technology she is developing." Ingrams looked at Michael with disgust.

Emma found her voice. "Why don't you just get me protection then if you're that worried someone will force me to tell what I know?"

"You haven't been trained, Ms. Welby. One fingernail. That's all it would take to make you talk."

"Really? I seem to remember you beating the crap out of me, and I didn't say a word about Michael." She grinned at his smug face.

She was goading Ingrams and was going to get them shot sooner rather than later, Michael thought. He squeezed her hand and looked in her eyes, pleading with her to shut her mouth. "Emma, I will handle this," Michael demanded, hoping she would forgive him for taking the lead.

He had to get her to keep quiet. Her voice irritated Ingrams. Michael could read it on his face, the way his beady little eyes bunched up at her words, the way he drew his lips into a taut line, the way the vein bulged in his neck.

It was a good thing Michael was experienced at thinking fast on his feet. Michael suddenly stood, throwing Ingrams off guard. Ingrams, still seated in the plush brown chair that resided in the corner of her living room, quickly raised his gun to Michael. Michael slowly moved forward. Ingrams did not have the training Michael had. Michael had to train for two years before he made Green Beret. Ingrams was nowhere near his level.

Michael slowly advanced on Ingrams.

"Stay where you are. I will kill you here, although I had other plans." Ingrams re-aimed his gun at Emma.

Michael gradually moved ever so slightly to position himself between Ingrams and Emma. But Ingrams still had the gun. Michael continued his gradual advance.

"I said *stop*!" Ingrams bellowed with such determination that Michael actually stopped.

He was walking on thin ice. Ingrams would kill him if he couldn't get that gun away from him. Ingrams stood, and in two strides, was just out of Michael's reach. He kept the gun on his biggest threat, Michael.

"We are going for a little ride. Ms. Welby, you drive." Ingrams said, never breaking eye contact with Michael. This was a showdown. He knew if Michael got within arm's reach, he could disarm him. Michael stayed his ground as Ingrams advanced a step.

Emma stood. Michael guided Emma to stand behind him. Reaching for his arm, she followed and pressed her front against Michael's back. Michael had to do something. He advanced on Ingrams. He was going to end this now, before anyone got hurt. All he needed was a slight distraction, something to draw Ingrams' eyes away from him for just a second. It was at the exact moment, almost like she could read his mind, that Emma took a sideways step from behind Michael.

There it was. Ingrams glanced at Emma. Michael threw himself at Ingrams, bending Ingrams' wrist sideways, hoping he would loosen his grip and drop the gun. Michael brought up his knee in one swift movement and, at the same time, pulled Ingrams down. Michael rammed his knee into Ingrams' stomach, causing him to hunch over. Michael continued his assault. He grabbed Ingram's hand and pushed it high over his head so Ingrams couldn't get off a shot. He connected his right hook to Ingrams' jaw. Ingrams stumbled backwards a step. He wrestled with all his might to bring the gun back down and point it at Michael. He had almost succeeded. Just then, Emma tackled Ingrams from the side, falling with him to the floor. Michael no longer had a hold of Ingrams. Emma was lying on top of him, vulnerable, exposed.

Ingrams brought the gun up and Emma, knowing the very real threat, fought for her life. Emma was screaming at the top of her lungs, although she didn't recognize the sound as her own. She grabbed a hold of his hand, trying to wrestle the gun from him. She used all her body weight to keep the gun from pointing at her chest. She rested fully on Ingrams' hands with her body and managed to turn the gun to the side so it was no longer pointed at her chest. It was pure adrenaline flowing through her blood that gave her the strength.

Michael stood motionless, in shock at the sight that was playing out before him. The thought of losing Emma paralyzed him. "Mess with the best and die like the rest"—his motto during those long two years of training—kicked in. He took two steps and bent forward to wrestle the gun from Ingrams' hand. In this position, with Ingrams on the floor, Michael had the upper hand. But the gun was buried somewhere between two bodies.

He heard the shot. He looked down and neither Ingrams nor Emma were moving. Blood pooled on the floor. He had failed again. He was going to kill the bastard. Michael scrambled on his knees to feel Ingrams' neck. No pulse! He stood, picking Emma up from Ingrams' dead body and wrapped her safely in his arms. He walked her over to the couch and gently laid her down. He felt her neck to make sure. A pulse, thank God!

He trekked back over to Ingrams' body. The blood was starting to spread to Emma's nice white, shag carpet—turning the edges red. Michael looked for the entrance wound. He had to give it to his girl. She had guts. She had managed to shoot him sideways through the heart. The exit wound was on Ingrams' lower side. Michael had no idea how she was able to overpower Ingrams. Ingrams wasn't a large man, but he thought his Emma was no match for him. Apparently, Emma isn't so delicate, he thought.

He heard movement from the couch. Confident their nemesis was dead, he made his way over to Emma.

"What happened?" she asked, confused.

"You did it. You took him down, Emma. I am so proud of you," Michael cooed praise into her ear while he stroked her hair.

Emma started crying, loud heaving sobs racking her body.

"What's the matter?" Michael inquired, concern lacing his voice.

"I took a life!" she screamed.

Her first kill, of course. He had long since forgotten the feeling of taking a human's life.

"I was looking right in his eyes before . . ."

"It's okay, Emma. Either you were going to die or he was. You did what you had to do. I know exactly how you feel. Your adrenaline is flowing free and fast right now. You can't blame yourself. You have to keep telling yourself it was you or him. You didn't want to kill him. Hell, if he hadn't shown up here, he would still be alive."

Her hands were shaking, and her body trembled.

"My hands burn, Michael," she admitted, calming herself a little.

"It's just from the heat of the gunfire. Here, let me have a look," he said, gathering her hands in his.

He opened her hands, palm up. Sure enough, there were red burn marks from the hold she had on the barrel of the gun. He gathered her into his arms and rocked her back and forth until her sobbing ceased.

CLOSER

"Okay, Kevin. Thank you," Michael said as he disconnected from the call.

The police were swarming through her apartment. They had yellow tape over the door and wouldn't allow either of them to leave. After all, she had a dead CIA agent in her living room.

Emma was still in shock. She was answering the questions the detectives threw at her the best she could, but she was emotionless. Michael had never seen her so drained of life. He was deeply concerned for her emotional well-being. He knew she was strong physically, but how strong was she emotionally?

"So he was here when you showed up?" the detective asked in disbelief. "Why would a man of his rank want to kill you?"

"I'm telling you the truth. Contact Brigadier General Landen. He'll tell you all about my project. He'll confirm that I am telling you the truth," she calmly told the detective.

But she had killed a man. She felt in some way she deserved to be punished for taking a life. The guilt was overwhelming her. She began to cry again.

Immediately, Michael stopped talking to the other detective and was at her side.

"I think she's had enough for one day, don't you? Make your phone calls. Call this number. He is with Homeland Security. He's familiar with the situation and can help clear up this matter." Michael placed one arm around Emma, tucking her neatly into his side while he handed Kevin's card to the detective. He made it clear she wasn't going anywhere, with anyone, tonight.

The forensics team arrived to remove the body. They took many pictures and then loaded the body onto a gurney. Thankfully, Ingrams was finally removed from her apartment.

"Johnny, I want pictures of the burns on her hands." The detective turned towards Michael and Emma. "I guess that's all for tonight. But don't leave town. We'll want you to come down to the station first thing in the morning." The detective told her in no uncertain terms that she wasn't off the hook yet. She would probably face charges for killing Ingrams.

"I don't want to stay here, Michael," Emma whispered. She turned her head to her side to inhale his unique scent.

"Of course not, baby. We'll stay at my place tonight. We'll get some guys to come and clean the place tomorrow. After they're done, you won't even be able to tell anything happened here at all," he reassured her.

"I don't ever want to stay here again, Michael. I'll have to find another place," she said more to herself than to him.

Michael hugged her tightly against his body. "Let's just worry about tonight. We'll worry about everything else tomorrow. Deal?" he asked, kissing the top of her head.

"Deal," she said, leaning into his kiss.

It was after dark by the time they arrived at his one-bedroom apartment. Upon walking in the door, he instantly regretted the way he used to live. A scotch bottle still sat next to his recliner. He hurried to remove the clothes strewn about so she could sit down on the couch.

"It's not as nice as either of your places. I've been saving my money to buy a cabin in the Sugarloaf Mountains, like yours," he explained, his face reddening with embarrassment. He couldn't ever remember blushing before, and he wasn't doing it now because he was ashamed of who he was. He was just ashamed of how he had lived the last six months of his life. Emma had brought him back to life. He wanted to enjoy it and take part in fully living again with her at his side.

"You've got to be starving. I'm gonna make us something light. It's late, and I'm not sure your stomach will do so well with a heavy meal," he told her as he walked into the kitchen and opened the cupboard. He found a can of Spaghetti-o's. I can't feed her this, he thought. He hadn't been to his place in weeks; everything in the fridge had gone bad. "How 'bout we order some take-out. Do you like Chinese?" he asked, bringing a menu to her.

She nodded and said, "You order. I will eat whatever."

She couldn't think about food right now, not with the thought of killing a man still in her head. She needed Michael to somehow make it all go away.

The food arrived, and Michael arranged it on two plates. He placed her plate on his coffee table because he didn't have a kitchen table. She picked up the plate, rested it on her knees, which were pulled tightly to her chest, and pushed her food around the plate.

"Tell me how to help you, Emma. I hate seeing you like this," Michael said, pleading with her.

If only she knew how he could make it all go away. She set her plate back on the coffee table. She took Michael's plate from his hands and placed it next to hers. She moved so she was straddling Michael. "Make me forget, Michael. Take it away," she pleaded, looking into his sexy caramel eyes lined with thick, dark lashes.

She placed a kiss on his neck. Then another one. She ran her tongue from the base of his neck to his earlobe. She whispered, "Make love to me."

Michael went instantly hard. She felt him pressing against her clit. She rubbed herself against his hard shaft unabashedly. She continued nipping and kissing his neck.

His hands found their way under her shirt. He worked to remove her bra. He finally released the clasp on the front. She sat up straight and peeled her shirt over her head. Then she removed her bra. She leaned back in so she could continue licking the sweet salt from his neck. She inhaled deeply, relaxing in his particular scent. He found her breasts and grasped each one. He pinched both of her nipples hard, gauging her reaction. She screamed at the pain then melted in the pleasure. She rubbed herself harder against him through his jeans.

Michael thought she needed it rough tonight to make her forget. Tonight was about her being his. He left her breast and moved his hand into the back of her hair. He pulled hard, and she moaned low in her throat. He knew exactly what her body needed, because this was what he needed after he had killed someone—pain.

Emma liked the exquisite pain that lasted seconds until it morphed into nothing but pleasure.

He roughly pulled her back from him by her hair. She met his eyes and he saw fire dancing in them. He bit her shoulder hard, so hard he left teeth marks. She rewarded him by pulling against his hand to kiss him. Her kiss was ravaged with need and desire. She ached in every pore of her being for him. She kissed him wildly. She was out of control. Her tongue sought his. She pushed into his mouth and explored like he had done to her many times.

Michael pushed back until he possessed her mouth. He was only going to let her think she had control. "Remove your clothes," he commanded.

She stood and dropped her pants and panties to the floor in one swoop.

He stood and said, "Undress me."

She followed his orders and ripped his shirt open, the buttons popping and flying in every direction. There was nothing gentle about her tonight. She leaned in and bit his nipple, hard, like the way he had bit her shoulder. He winced at the pain, but then she took it away by flicking her tongue over it and then sucking it into her mouth.

She pushed him back down on the couch and covered his lap with hers, straddling him. She positioned his cock at the entrance of her pussy. She bent forward, bit his neck hard, and slammed down on his cock, burying him deep inside her. They both growled at the feeling of him being fully sheathed by her. She took pleasure in the fullness of her pussy, the way her walls stretched to accommodate his length and girth. He placed his hands on her hips and guided her up and down over his cock, meeting each of her downward movements with one of his own upward ones.

"Harder," she pleaded.

Their bodies meshed together, forming one. They rode the wave in unison, kissing and biting each other. Hands explored flesh. Each time he would pinch her nipple with his fingers, she would reward him by moving back and forth over his pubic bone, taking him deeper than he had ever known. She rode him hard. She impaled herself with him. He brought his open palm down over her ass and spanked her. The first one was just an easy smack to see how she would react. When she threw her head back in pleasure and called his name, he satisfied her with another smack to her ass, this one much harder than the first. So hard his hand was tingling.

Michael's smack had hurt, but the burn soon melted into pleasure. She rode him harder. Higher and higher. He hit her other cheek even harder.

"More," she begged.

He lifted her from him and said, "Get on your knees."

She practically came at his command. She knelt on the uncomfortable carpet as he joined her. He took her hips possessively in his hands and thrust deep inside her, bringing her back against him as he thrust forward. He withdrew completely. He left one hand on her hip but slapped her ass with the other hand.

This slap made her scream, "More!"

She felt the burn of pain, but it soon morphed into a fire of pleasure. Her voice was hoarse as she pleaded to be punished. He commanded, "Stand up."

Michael sat on the couch and motioned for her to lie across his lap. She did so willingly. He took her over his knee and spanked her ass in an upward stroke again and again. With each smack, she climbed towards orgasm. She angled her ass so his slaps would hit just the right spot. Her behind was red from his ministrations. He took care not to smack her in the same place twice. He knew she couldn't take much more. He slapped her ass again, taking care to hit the spot that connected between her thighs. He did so again and again as she cried out his name. She quivered against him, her orgasm shaking her to the core. Now he'd get to see that beautiful, tamed red ass as he fucked her. He waited until she was done coming down from her high before he ordered, "Back on your knees."

She found her same spot on the carpet. Her ass was on fire with pleasure. She had never been spanked before, but she knew she needed it. He positioned himself to take her and that's what he did. He thrust into her over and over again with a fever she had never felt before. He was fucking her hard. She felt him deep inside to the point where it was almost painful. But he managed to make his fucking pleasurable, stroking her walls with his cock each time he withdrew.

Michael gently rubbed her ass with his hand, admiring the ways he had marked her as his. It was too much—the sight of his markings, the feel of her pussy around his cock. With one more thrust he fell forward with his own release. It was enough to send her into another orgasm. She sucked at his cock as he pumped his hips into her a few more times, squirting his hot liquid inside her tight pussy.

She felt their juices run down her legs when he pulled his semi-hard dick out of her swollen flesh.

"Stand up," he ordered. She obeyed. He lifted her into his arms and carried her to his bedroom.

"Let's get a shower before bed," he said as he placed her on her feet. Her legs trembled from coming so hard.

He took care in the shower to wash every inch of her body. He took special care to wash her ass. After the shower, he dried her and asked her to lie down in his bed, backside up. He came to her side with cream that would help the burn. He had really given it to her. He didn't want her to feel pain, only pleasure. He gently rubbed the cream into her skin. When he was done, he left the bed and returned to the bathroom. When he reemerged, he heard her cute little snore. She was sound asleep. He crawled into bed behind her and pulled her close to him. She snuggled in and he fell fast asleep—all demons exorcised.

CLOSER

The ringing of Michael's cell phone awakened him. It was after 0800 hours. He couldn't remember the last time he'd slept that late. He didn't want to wake Emma, so he removed her from his arms carefully and found his phone. "Hello?" Michael said, recognizing Kevin's number from the caller ID.

"Look. I wanted to be the one to tell you that, apparently, Agent Ingrams had an impressive record. But lately his boss noted he was obsessed with the GIA," Kevin said in a calm voice, like Michael's whole world wasn't depending on the outcome of this investigation.

"And . . ." Michael hissed at his brother.

"And the PD's forensics department confirmed her burn marks were consistent with her story. She wrestled the gun from him and it went off." He smiled, knowing his brother was smiling on the other end.

"So, that's it. It's over. No more questions?" Michael asked cautiously not wanting to get his hopes up.

"Oh, I'm sure there will be some more questions, but she is cleared of any wrongdoing. The PD concluded it was a case of self-defense," Kevin said.

Michael exhaled.

"Are you okay, man? I thought this would be good news," Kevin said, still smiling.

"This is the best news I have heard in a long, long time."

"I just wanted to be the one to tell you. Go, enjoy that girl of yours."

"I plan on it," Michael confirmed before ending the call. He couldn't wait to tell her. He knew it was weighing on her mind. He carefully crawled back into bed with her. She snuggled back into his arms. This is exactly where she belongs for the rest of her life, Michael thought.

He had more than one piece of good news to share this morning. He just hoped she was ready for it all because he was done fighting with his feelings. He loved her. He wanted her with him forever.

She turned and faced him. He brushed the hair from her eyes as she peeked out from sleep. His smile was the first thing she saw.

"Well, good morning to you, too," she smiled in return.

Michael pulled her closer until their noses were touching. He rubbed his nose with hers. She giggled.

"How are you feeling this morning, Emma?" he inquired, gazing into her beautifully blue eyes.

"I am much better after last night. Thank you, Michael. You took it away," she confessed.

"You don't have to ever thank me for that. Believe me, I enjoyed taming that beautiful ass, marking it as mine."

It was now or never. He had to tell her. His tone changed into a serious one. "I have to tell you something."

She propped herself up on her elbow, determined to hear the bad news with dignity. "What is it?" she asked, her eyes quickly darting from his. She bit her bottom lip as she waited for the dreaded news.

"I think I am falling in love with you," he said.

Her eyes shot up and connected with his. He was worried. She wasn't saying anything back yet. She just stared at him like she was lost.

"It's okay if you don't feel the same way, Emma. You don't have to. I know it has been quick. And we didn't exactly meet under normal circumstances. And the last few weeks have been crazy, but they also have been the best weeks of my life. I don't want to lose you. So you take all the time . . ."

"Michael," she said. "Shut up and kiss me."

She pulled him down into the most sweet, most tender kiss. They lied in bed kissing each other, connecting with each other for an hour, just kissing and touching each other's faces.

When she finally pulled away, she gathered up her courage and said, "I am in love with you. But . . ."

"No buts," he demanded.

This time she disobeyed. "But what about Ingrams? I may get in a lot of trouble for what I did," she protested as she fought back the tears. She had finally found love, and it could all just disappear.

"Well," he said. "I have something else to tell you." He didn't even try to hide his smile. Apparently, it was infectious because she started smiling, too, although she had no idea why.

"Out with it," she said as she tickled his ribs.

He started laughing. When she finished her assault on his ribs, he finally was able to calm down.

"Kevin called. He wanted to be the one to tell me the good news," Michael declared.

"What good news?" She eyed him suspiciously with a twinkle in her eye.

He laced his hands through her soft hair and pulled her in for another kiss.

She backed away. "No. No. Tell me," she admonished.

"The police have ruled Ingrams' death self-defense. Apparently the burns on your hands corroborated our story. You are officially . . . all mine," he declared.

"So what does this mean? Will you take me on a regular date?" she teased.

"It means you don't need to look for a place to live. You can live here with me during the week, and we will live at your cabin during the weekends. That is, of course, if you want to," he said with trepidation.

"Isn't it a little fast? We have only known each other a short time," she argued.

"Look, if you don't want to, that's fine. I was just throwing it out there because you don't want to live at your place in the city anymore," he said, sounding dejected. His eyes roamed the room for a moment, not connecting with hers.

She brushed his stubbly cheek with her fingers, enjoying the feel of it against her skin. "Michael, I would love to move in with you. In fact, if you didn't ask, I would have been heartbroken," she confided.

"So we're really doing this? You're in love with me and moving in?" He had to hear her say it again.

She smiled. "Yes, Michael. I am hopelessly in love with you. And I'm moving in with you. But you are also moving in with me. The cabin is more like my home. Will you live with me there?"

"You know, Emma, we're sitting on a nice little nest egg now that I don't have to buy a cabin." He smiled.

"Good, then let's find an apartment in the city that won't be yours and won't be mine, but will be ours. This one will be too small for the both of us." She kissed him, melting into his touch.

He caressed her exposed arm with his fingertips. He rolled her over onto her back and pressed against her entrance with his hardness. Her blood was on fire. He pushed into her slowly, kissing her reverently. She kissed him back, allowing herself to fall even deeper for the man. She was consumed by him. He slowly moved in and out of her. She was his, and she felt much love and confidence in that knowledge. There were no more bad guys. Although she didn't know it, she had vanquished his demons.

As he made love to her, she realized Michael understood her barest needs. That realization brought her closer to her climax. She finally came, clenching her muscles as she dissolved into Michael. With one more thrust, he followed. He lay on her, inside her, not wanting to move and spoil such a perfect union.

He whispered, "Tell me you're mine, forever."

"I'm yours, forever."

The End

SARAH GREYSON

I want to hear from you. To contact me, follow one of the following links.

Email: Sarah@SarahGreyson.com
Website: https://www.sarahgreyson.com
Amazon Author page: http://www.amazon.com/-/e/B00L99CNY2
aboutme: http://about.me/sarahgreyson
Google+: http://bit.ly/GooglePlusSarahGreyson
Twitter: https://twitter.com/Sarah_G_Greyson
Facebook: http://bit.ly/SarahGreysonsFacebookPage
Pinterest: http://www.pinterest.com/Greysonnovels/
Tumblr: http://sarahgreyson.tumblr.com/

www.ingramcontent.com/pod-product-compliance
Lightning Source LLC
Chambersburg PA
CBHW070654180626
46817CB00006B/2360